THE TWISTS AND TURNS OF LOVE

A Regency Romance

How strange that a carriage accident could bring such enchantment into Petula's life.

Buried in the country, she was completely unused to such witty or handsome company as Major Adrian Chester. What good fortune that he was forced to spend the night at the manor house. And what a marvelous evening they spent together.

The morning brought still greater delight:

"I could not sleep for thinking about you," the Major said and suddenly his lips were on hers.

The kiss was so wonderful, so perfect, that Petula felt as if they were alone in a secret place far removed from the world. She thought he would kiss her again, but then he said abruptly:

"I have to be on my way as soon as possible."

Would the enchantment end now . . . forever?

BARBARA CARTLAND

Bantam Books by Barbara Cartland
Ask your bookseller for the books you have missed

Barbara Cartland's Library of Love

Barbara Cartland

The Twists and Turns of Love

BANTAM BOOKS · TORONTO · NEW YORK · LONDON

THE TWISTS AND TURNS OF LOVE
A Bantam Book/February 1978

ISBN 0-553-11797-1

Published simultaneously in the United States and Canada

Bantam Books are published by Bantam Books, Inc. Its trade-
mark, consisting of the words "Bantam Books" and the por-
trayal of a bantam, is registered in the United States Patent
Office and in other countries. Marca Registrada. Bantam
Books, Inc., 666 Fifth Avenue, New York, New York 10019.

PRINTED IN THE UNITED STATES OF AMERICA

Author's Note

In the 1800s, gambling losses and gains ran into astronomic figures among the Bucks in the London Clubs. Charles James Fox, a compulsive gambler, would play for twenty-fours hours at a sitting, losing five hundred pounds an hour.

To achieve present-day values we should multiply the sum by approximately twenty. In this story, Sir Roderick would have won over one hundred thousand pounds.

The Royal Drawing-Rooms which Queen Charlotte held every Thursday were altered to Evening Courts by Edward VII. I was presented at one in 1925, and at another in 1928 after my marriage.

In 1939, just before the outbreak of war, both Drawing-Rooms and Levees were discontinued.

Chapter One
1802

The gentleman walking down the rough gravel drive with its innumerable pot-holes slipped in his polished Hessians.

He swore under his breath and cursed himself again for having taken the wrong turn and landing up with a buckled wheel of his Phaeton.

It was his own fault, he thought, and he had no-one else to blame.

He had left London late, after spending the night with a fair Charmer who was so entrancingly seductive that she made him forget the long journey that was waiting for him the following morning.

He had, however, driven very fast and his new team of chestnuts had excelled themselves.

Even so, it had meant that he had spent his first night nearer London than he had intended, while on the second he had arrived later than was polite at the mansion of a friend, where he had arranged to stay the night.

This meant that out of sheer courtesy it was impossible for him to leave as soon as he had finished breakfast.

There had been horses to inspect and a number of gallant exchanges with his hostess and her plain

1

daughters before finally he could be on the road again.

He had been told of a short-cut which involved turning off the main highway and now he knew it had been not only a mistake but a disaster.

Driving at what he admitted was a dangerous speed along a narrow lane, at a blind corner he had encountered a farm wagon.

Only by the most skilful driving had he prevented a head-on clash between his horses and an aged farm animal.

Nevertheless, a wheel of his Phaeton had come into contact with one of the wagon wheels and it was impossible for him to proceed farther.

The yokel had suggested that he might find help at the Manor House. So, leaving his groom in charge of his team, the gentleman had passed through a pair of dilapidated gates to find himself in a drive which he felt could not have been repaired for at least a hundred years!

It was in fact extremely picturesque, with the rhododendron, lilac, and syringa bushes which bordered it all overgrown with a riot of blossoms.

The gentleman, however, was concerned not with beauty but with getting his Phaeton back on the road.

He strode on as fast as he could along the drive, thinking that when it rained the resulting morass of mud and puddles would make it impassable.

Suddenly there was a turn in the drive and he found himself looking at the Manor House which he was seeking.

At first glance it was rather attractive.

Originally Tudor, he thought, but the creeper which grew all over it made it hard to distinguish its actual period.

There was a gravel sweep in front of the house which was in the same condition of disrepair as the drive, and again there was a riot of shrubs, brilliant against what could be seen of the ancient, weather-beaten bricks.

Looking at the house, the Marquis also noted that many of the top windows were apparently boarded up.

Even on the first and ground floors, panes of glass were missing and had been replaced either with wood or cardboard.

The front door, which was badly in need of a coat of paint, was shut, but under the creeper growing round it there was a bell-pull, and a brass knocker which had once been shiny but was now black and broken.

The gentleman tried both and waited.

Nothing happened and he thought it more than likely that the occupants of the house were away from home.

He decided he would try the back door.

He walked round the house and saw through an opening in an ancient red brick wall a kitchen-garden in which two people were working.

That, he thought, was more promising, and he walked towards the nearer of them. One was a woman wearing a faded cotton gown and a sun-bonnet on her head.

She was planting seeds, bending over a long line marked in a small patch of ground which had recently been dug.

The gentleman walked up to her.

"I wish," he said in an authoritative voice, "to speak to the owner of the house, but I find it impossible to get any answer at the front door."

At the sound of his voice the woman started and straightened her back, and he found himself looking at the face of a girl.

She was undoubtedly young and she was also exceedingly lovely.

The eyes that looked enquiringly into his seemed unnaturally large in the shade of her sun-bonnet and were the deep blue of the periwinkles that he had seen growing in profusion amongst the uncut grass beside the drive.

3

For a moment the girl seemed too surprised to speak, but when she did her voice was soft and cultured.

"I am sorry," she said. "The bell is broken, and if Annie was in the kitchen she would not have heard the knocker."

Instinctively, because he realised she was not what he had first thought, the gentleman raised his hat.

"Am I speaking to the owner of the house?" he asked.

"You are!" she replied simply.

"Then I have come to you for help," the gentleman said. "I have had an accident with my Phaeton in a narrow lane about a quarter of a mile from your gates, and I need a wheelwright."

"No-one is hurt, I hope?" the girl asked quickly.

"No, it was not a bad accident," he replied, "but it prevents me from going any farther, and I am, as it happens, in a hurry."

The girl to whom he was speaking was, he realised, looking at him with an undoubted expression of admiration on her face. Rather belatedly he realised he had been somewhat peremptory in voicing his request.

"My name," he said, "is Chester—Major Adrian Chester—and I am on my way to Kirkby Castle."

"My name is Petula Buckden," the girl replied, "and I expect you know already that this is Buckden Manor."

"I gathered that was the name of the village from the rather half-witted yokel who directed me here."

She glanced at him swiftly as if she was surprised at the tone of his voice.

"That, I imagine, will be Ned, if he was driving the wagon."

"He was," Major Chester admitted, "and in case you are worrying, I can assure you that both Ned and the wagon are unscathed."

He spoke in a sarcastic tone which brought a flush of colour to Petula's cheeks.

She put down on the ground the seeds she was holding in a basin and walked towards an elderly man who was working farther down the garden.

"Adam!" she called. "This gentleman needs Ben to repair a wheel. Do you know where he will be?"

The man to whom she was speaking dug his spade into the ground and came slowly towards her.

"Ye be askin' for Ben, Miss Petula?"

"Yes, Adam."

" 'E'll be up with Farmer Jarvis if 'e ain't gone nowhere else."

"Will you go and find him?" Petula asked. "Tell him there has been an accident."

"It'll take Oi some time t' walk t' th' farm, Miss Petula."

"Then you had better take the gig," Petula said. "Bessie has been out this morning, so take her slowly. She is getting too old for two journeys a day."

"Oi'll do that, Miss."

Adam went back to collect his spade, moving at a rate which made the Major tap his foot impatiently and repress an inclination to assert once again that he was in a hurry.

"It is doubtful if Ben could be here in under an hour," Petula said. "Perhaps you would like to bring your horses into the stables? If the wheel is badly bent Ben will need to take it to his workshop."

"Where is that?" Major Chester asked in the tone of one who expects to hear the worst.

"It is at the other end of the village."

"I might have guessed it!"

Petula laughed.

"I am afraid you will find in Buckden, as in most small places in Yorkshire, that what we do we do well, but it takes time."

The Major drew his watch from his waist-coat pocket.

"It is after three-thirty P.M.," he said. "How long do you think it will take me to get from here to Kirkby Castle?"

"I am afraid I have no idea," Petula answered. "Several hours, at least."

She knew that Kirkby Castle was the home of the Earl of Kirkby, who was Lord Lieutenant of Yorkshire.

"It looks to me," the Major said, "as if I am going to be extremely late, if I arrive at all. Is there an Inn nearby?"

"Not one at which you can stay, and certainly not one in which you could stable your horses."

For a moment the Major looked at Petula almost angrily, as if it were her fault that the accommodation was so inadequate. Then he smiled.

It transformed his face, and while before she had thought him a cold and autocratic type, she realised now that he also had charm.

She had in fact been overwhelmed by his appearance.

Never had she imagined that any gentleman could be so elegantly dressed and at the same time look so extremely masculine.

She realised that his white cravat was an intricate masterpiece and that the points of his collar, which reached slightly above his square chin, were the very latest fashion for a Beau.

She noted too how well his grey whipcord fitted over his shoulders, and as he was still standing, with his hat in his hand, she was sure that his hair was cut in the fashion that had been set by the Prince of Wales.

However, because she felt rather humbled by his magnificence and was well aware that in contrast she looked shabby and what she described in her own mind as "a mess," she said shyly:

"If you would like to fetch your horses I will see that the stables are emptied of anything that has been stored there. We only have Bessie now and she is out in the fields at this time of the year."

"I would not wish to put you to any trouble," the Major said. "And I am hoping that when the wheelwright can be found my journey will not be long delayed."

Petula did not answer. He thought that his hopes were unlikely to be realised and he must make the best of the situation, infuriating though it was.

He therefore followed her as she walked towards a building at the back of the house, which he realised contained the stables.

They were in what the Major privately thought a most disgraceful state of repair. Tiles were off the roof, leaving great holes which undoubtedly let in the rain.

When Petula pulled open one of the doors he saw that there had once been stabling for a dozen horses and the stalls were intact. However, they were dusty and dirty, and the spiders had spun their webs from bar to bar.

"You are driving a pair, I suppose?" Petula asked.

"No, four," Major Chester replied briefly.

Her eyes lit up.

"I have never travelled behind a four-in-hand," she said. "It must be exciting to move so fast!"

"It is, when one is travelling," the Major replied.

As he spoke he realised that he was being ungracious, but he was still feeling angry not only at the delay but at being involved in an accident through his own fault.

He should not have left the main road; he should not have travelled so fast down a country lane. But what was the use of going over it all again?

He had better make the best of a bad job and be thankful that at any rate there was a wheelwright within reach.

In the stables there were fortunately four stalls

7

that were not cluttered with old implements, pack-ing-cases, and logs of wood.

"Adam will bring in some straw when he comes back," Petula said. "I am afraid your horses will not be very comfortable, but at least they can rest."

"You are extremely kind, Miss Buckden, and I am grateful," the Major said.

"Perhaps before you fetch the horses you would like some refreshment?" Petula suggested. "There is some cider in the house, or tea if you prefer."

"I would find a glass of cider most acceptable," the Major said politely.

Petula led the way round from the stables to-wards the front of the house.

Despite her shabby and faded cotton gown, the man walking beside her realised that she moved with a lithe grace which he had not expected in a countrywoman.

His host's daughters of the previous evening had been thick-set and ungainly.

In his mind he described them as being "clumpy" and found himself remembering the movements of the Charmer who had made him late in starting on his journey.

'God deliver me from a woman whose foot is heavy as she crosses the floor,' he had thought.

Petula seemed to float rather than walk, and when she opened the front door and entered the cool, low-ceilinged hall, she undid the ribbons of her sun-bonnet.

She took it off as naturally as a man might re-move his hat upon entering a house.

It was then that Major Chester told himself that she was as unexpectedly lovely as an orchid growing on a rubbish heap.

Never before could he remember seeing hair that appeared almost like a shaft of sunshine against the dark panelling of the hall, and her complexion was as pink and white as the blossoms on the almond trees outside.

She carried her head poudly on a long neck that
was as graceful as her movements, and there was just
a faint touch of amusement in her voice as she said:

"Perhaps you would not mind waiting in the
Drawing-Room while I fetch the cider for you? I am
afraid there is no-one else in the house except my old
Nurse."

"I do not wish to put you to any trouble, Miss
Buckden," the Major replied.

"It is no trouble," Petula answered automatically.

She opened the door of the Drawing-Room and
he entered, looking abnormally tall and broad-shoul-
dered, then she ran down the long passage which
led to the kitchen.

The house, which really needed at least a dozen
servants to look after it, was hopelessly large for just
herself and Annie.

They found that the only way they could manage was to shut up every room that was not needed
and try to keep clean only the ones which were essential.

Petula found Annie, as she had expected, in the
kitchen baking bread, which she did once a week.

"Your tea's not ready yet, Miss Petula," she said
without looking up, "so it's no use your a-bothering
me for a crust from a hot loaf, and I knows that's
what you're after!"

"You are mistaken, Annie!" Petula replied. "It is
a flagon of cider of which I am in need."

"Cider?" Annie cried. "If Adam thinks he's having
cider at this time in the afternoon he's mistaken!"

"It is not for Adam," Petula said as she took a
glass jug and a tumbler out of a cupboard. "We have
a visitor."

"A visitor?" Annie exclaimed. "That's a change!
Is it the Vicar?"

"No, Annie. It is the most magnificent gentleman
you have ever seen. There has been an accident to
the wheel of his Phaeton and he ran into Ned's wagon."

"Then I'll bet that lazy Ned was asleep as usual!"

Annie said sharply. "They've no right to let him drive when he's no idea in which direction he's a-going."

"The horse knows its own way home," Petula laughed, "and I have a shrewd suspicion, although I would not dare voice it to him, that the gentleman was travelling too fast."

"There's never a gentleman as doesn't do that," Annie replied, "as I said to your father often enough, when he was alive."

"Papa seldom had good horse-flesh to drive," Petula answered.

There was a little sob in her voice as she spoke and her eyes misted.

It was hard now, after nearly five months, to think of her father without crying and it was still an agony to be without him.

She went into the cool larder which led off the kitchen.

There was little enough nowadays to put on the wide marble slabs. She could remember that in her grandfather's day there were huge open bowls of cream, big pats of yellow butter, and wicker baskets filled with brown eggs.

Now there were only a few eggs from the hens which Annie treasured, which were eaten only on special occasions, and a jug of milk that Adam collected every morning from the adjacent farm.

There were under one of the slabs three large stone flagons of home-made cider, which were kept for occasional visitors and for Adam.

It was part of his wages, her father had always said, and although Annie sniffed and said they could not afford it, Petula insisted that Adam was entitled to his daily glass of cider.

The flagons were refilled as soon as they were empty, and she tipped one cautiously, since it was very heavy, until she had filled the glass jug which she had set down on the flagged floor.

Carrying it back to the kitchen, she put it on the

silver salver which Annie had fetched from another cupboard and placed the tumbler beside it.

"It's a good thing I cleaned the silver two days ago," Annie remarked. "I kept putting it off until I was ashamed to look at it."

"I am sure our guest will be impressed at how well it shines," Petula said.

Actually she felt that nothing in the Manor was likely to impress the Major favourably. At the same time, it was rather exciting to have a visitor. Often weeks passed by and she saw no-one except Annie and Adam.

Then she would make an excuse to go to the village simply because it was pleasant to chat with Mr. Yarrow, the butcher, or Mrs. Blackburn, at the Crown and Feathers.

It was only as she was walking back towards the Drawing-Room that Petula thought of her own appearance and wondered if she should have gone upstairs and put on a better gown than the one she was wearing.

But she told herself it was unlikely that Major Chester would notice her at all, and if he did so it would be in the condescending manner in which he had spoken to her at first.

'He is obviously very puffed up with his own importance,' Petula thought. 'I expect he is wealthy. Rich men always seem to think the world is theirs to walk on.'

She carried the cider into the Drawing-Room and found that the Major was standing at the open window looking out over the uncut lawn.

The fields which bordered the garden sloped away towards a small wood, beyond which there was undulating countryside rising in the far distance to bare-topped hills.

"You have a very beautiful view from here, Miss Buckden," the Major said, turning to Petula as she walked towards him.

"I love it," Petula answered, "but then I have not seen many other places."

"You have lived here all your life?"

"Yes. There have been Buckdens in this house since the time of Queen Elizabeth, but they have never been great travellers."

The Major smiled as he poured himself out a glass of cider.

"I suppose by that remark you mean that you wish you could travel?"

"I would love to do so," Petula said, "and I am sure, now that the war is over, the people who have been confined to England during the war are hurrying to go abroad."

"That is true," the Major agreed, "but those like myself who have had enough of fighting are content to stay at home."

"You fought against Bonaparte?"

"For a short while," the Major replied, "but I was in India and took part in the wars there."

"How thrilling!"

There was no doubt that Petula was interested.

"I would love to hear about India. All the East sounds so fascinating. But perhaps that is only because I know so little about it."

"Parts of India are, as you say, fascinating," the Major said, "but it is also very hot, and war can be extremely uncomfortable."

He spoke in a dry voice which made Petula feel as if he had no wish to discuss it.

They therefore lasped into silence until the Major put down his tumbler and said:

"Thank you. The cider was very pleasant. Now, as you suggested, I had better fetch my horses and put them in the stable until the wheelwright tells me how long he will take repairing the Phaeton."

"I am afraid it will take Adam some time to reach the farm where we think he is working," Petula said apologetically.

She looked at the clock, then added:

"As I think it . . . unlikely that your wheel will be repaired before . . . dinner-time, would you like . . . something to eat before you proceed on your way?"

She spoke a little hesitantly because she was wondering almost wildly what they could offer him.

The Major also hesitated.

"I feel I have already put you to a great deal of trouble, Miss Buckden," he said. "Perhaps your local Inn will provide some sort of a meal for myself and my groom."

"It will only be bread and cheese," Petula said. "I am sure Annie could do better than that, although naturally it will not be the sort of fare to which you are accustomed."

"As a soldier I can assure you I have not always been well fed," the Major said with a smile, "and I shall be very grateful indeed, Miss Buckden, if I could avail myself of your hospitality before I set off on what will undoubtedly be a long and tiring drive."

"Then we will do our best," Petula said simply, "but please do not be too critical."

"I promise you I shall only be extremely grateful for your kindness," the Major answered.

Petula waited until he had left the house and was starting to walk back down the drive before she ran to the kitchen.

"Quick, Annie, quick!" she cried. "He is staying for dinner and his groom will also want something to eat."

"Staying for dinner? Whatever are you talking about, Miss Petula?"

"Major Chester. He had gone to fetch his horses to put them in the stables, and Adam has driven to Jarvis's to find Ben. He will be hours about it, as you know, and Ben will never hurry himself."

"You're expecting me to provide dinner, Miss Petula? With what, I ask you?"

Petula made a little gesture of helplessness.

"There must be something in the house, Annie!"

"There's a wee bit of lamb I was saving for your

13

luncheon tomorrow, Miss Petula, and there's a few eggs, but nothing else that I can recall."

Petula had gone to the larder door to look almost despairingly at the empty slabs. Then she gave a cry.

"There is a rabbit on the floor, Annie. Adam told me he caught it in a snare and was taking it home for his dog."

"Well that's better than nothing!" Annie said, and added: "His dog indeed! He'll eat it himself, the greedy pig, and us half-starving!"

"Adam works hard and he has to eat too!"

"Not our rabbits," Annie said harshly.

"If there is any left over you will have to give him some," Petula said soothingly. "After all, it was his snare, and if the rabbits belong to anyone they belong to him. We cannot claim what we cannot catch or shoot."

"I'm not arguing about it, Miss Petula," Annie said. "If Adam did as he was told there'd be a lot more to eat in this house than there is."

"At this time of the year . . ." Petula began to say.

Then she knew it was no use arguing with Annie.

Although she was country-born and -bred, she still persisted in believing that birds were plentiful all the year round and there was no breeding season to interfere with her larder of pigeons, partridges, and hares.

Petula gave her the rabbit and Annie set it down on the table. It was a young one but large enough to provide a meal unless the diner in question was very hungry.

"Here are the eggs, so you can make an omelette, Annie," Petula said.

"Using all my eggs!" Annie exclaimed in a note of horror. "Those were supposed to last you and me, Miss Petula, for several days!"

"I will look for nests you have not found," Petula promised. "And now I am going into the garden to find what vegetables we have."

As she reached the door she added:

"Thank goodness there are a few ripe plums on the south wall, which will do for desert. I know you have some cream hidden away."

"All I can say is that you and me, Miss Petula, will be going hungry for the rest of the week," Annie complained.

"We will manage somehow," Petula said, smiling as she ran off to the garden.

There was so much else to do that she felt she had hardly time to breathe before she saw Major Chester returning down the drive.

He was leading two horses and his groom behind him was leading another two, and the sight of them made Petula forget everything else.

Never in the whole of her life had she seen such magnificent animals or a team so perfectly matched.

With their long manes and tails, and with their chestnut coats seeming to shine in the sunshine, they looked, Petula thought, as if they had stepped from a painting by George Stubbs.

The Major led the way towards the stables and she followed them, noting that his groom wore an exceedingly smart livery with a crest on the silver buttons.

"I believe there is straw for them somewhere, Jason," the Major said, "but the man who was to provide it for us has gone in search of the wheelwright."

Before the groom could reply in what Petula was sure would be a supercilious manner she interrupted:

"It is stacked in the last stall and I will help you spread it."

"Certainly not!" the Major said sharply. "Jason will do that if you will show him where it is."

She knew that he was not only replying to her but was also giving an order to his groom.

She therefore walked to the end of the stables where the straw, which was to make a comfortable bed for Bessie during the winter, had been thrown down by the boy from the farm who brought it to them.

"It is here," Petula said.

The groom looked at it and to her surprise replied in a very pleasant tone:

"Thank you, Miss. Leave it to me. The horses won't want much, as we won't be staying long, but they could do with a drink."

"The pump is outside in the yard."

"Thank you, Miss."

She thought that the groom seemed more amenable than his master. Then, because she felt a little in awe of the Major, she asked tentatively:

"Was there ... any sign of Ben when you ... fetched your horses?"

"I thought, as you had already warned me that in this part of the country you make haste slowly, it would be a mistake to be too optimistic."

"He cannot be very much longer," Petula said.

Major Chester did not answer and she went on:

"Perhaps you would like to come to the house and rest? Dinner cannot be ready before another hour or so."

I certainly have no intention of walking any farther," the Major said, "and I suppose your man will know where to take the wheelwright."

"There is only one road into the village," Petula answered, "so it would be impossible for him to miss a Phaeton, a vehicle we do not often see."

She was not being sarcastic but she felt her visitor was being a little high-handed. Although she told herself it was childish, she rather resented his sneers at their slowness.

"Go back to the Phaeton, Jason," the Major said to his groom, "and fetch my valise. Then find out where this man, Ben, is taking the wheel and impress upon him the need for speed. Will there be a moon tonight?"

"No, not this week," Petula said before the groom could reply, "and I think you will find it difficult even with the lanterns on your Phaeton to find the way to Kirkby Castle."

"It will be light until about ten o'clock," the Major said almost as if he spoke to himself.

Petula knew he was calculating how soon the wheel was likely to be mended and, once it was, how far they would have to travel to the nearest Posting Inn.

"There is one at Huntingford," she said as if he had asked her the question. "It is about three or four miles after you get back onto the main road."

She saw the Major's lips tighten and after a moment in a nervous little voice she said:

"If it is . . . impossible for you to . . . get away tonight, we will . . . try to make you comfortable."

"You are very kind, Miss Buckden," the Major said, "but I am sure it will be quite unnecessary for for me to impose upon you any further."

Petula felt as if he had deliberately snubbed her. She walked out of the stable and back towards the house.

She had reached the front door before the Major caught up with her.

"You must forgive me," he said, "if I sounded somewhat abrupt and was not as profuse in my thanks for your offer of hospitality as I should have been. Quite frankly, I had not until that moment envisaged that I might not be able to get away tonight, but I do see now it may well be impossible."

He spoke with a warmth in his voice and a sincerity that had not been there before.

"I . . . quite understand," she said shyly. "I cannot offer you much but at least it is a roof over your head."

"I have a feeling," the Major said, "that I am behaving rather badly, like a spoilt child."

Petula laughed.

"Perhaps we all do that when we are disappointed. Was there a very exciting party waiting for you at Kirkby Castle?"

"I hope not!" the Major said fervently. "There is nothing more tiring than a large dinner-party with a crowd of strangers after you have just driven a great distance."

Petula, who had never been to a large dinner-party, thought it would in fact be a thrilling event however tiring the journey, but aloud she said:

"Instead you will have neither a large party nor a large dinner, but, as Annie has said ever since I was a child: 'What cannot be cured must be endured.'!"

It was the Major's turn to laugh.

"I can remember my Nurse saying exactly the same!"

"Mama told me they all have a language of their own."

They reached the hall and she added:

"I thought you might like to wash after driving so far, and I have put some warm water and towels in one of the bed-rooms."

"You think of everything, Miss Buckden," the Major said.

She went up the stairs, wondering as she did so if she had in fact remembered everything.

There had been the table to lay for dinner, the bed-room windows to open, water to be heated and taken upstairs, and a dozen other things that Annie asked for and could not cope with herself.

The room she had prepared for the Major was in fact her father's and had therefore not been shut up like most of the other bed-rooms on that floor.

She showed the Major into it and felt that although the carpet was shabby and the curtains faded it was a very pleasant room with its big four-poster bed, in which generation after generation of Buck-dens had been born and slept and died.

"I hope you will find all you need," Petula said nervously.

She was wondering if she should offer him her father's hair-brushes.

He must have guessed what she was thinking, because he said:

"My man is bringing me my valise from the Phae-ton, so I shall be self-sufficient."

Only as Petula hurried down the passage to her

18

own room did she wonder if the Major would have liked a bath.

But Annie could not have both heated the water and cooked the dinner, she told herself.

She reached her own room and only when she glanced in the mirror did she realise that she looked extremely untidy.

Her hair wanted brushing and was curling in riotous tendrils round her cheeks. Her gown, which was one of her older ones which she wore only to work in the garden, was creased and stained with earth from when she had been planting the seeds.

"He must think I am an absolute hooligan!" Petula exclaimed.

Pulling off her clothes, she washed in cold water, then went to her wardrobe.

There were not many gowns for her to choose from, because since her mother's death and her father's illness they had been so poor that she had never been able to afford a new one.

In fact she could not afford to go into mourning and so had gone on wearing her ordinary clothes, except that she added a black sash and black ribbons to her bonnet when she went to Church on Sundays.

"What can I wear?" she asked herself now.

Then she remembered that in a cupboard in her bed-room were all her mother's clothes.

She had always intended to use them because she longed to put on anything which had belonged to her mother, but there had been no occasion until now to wear anything but her own threadbare dresses.

Annie, if no-one else, would have thought it extremely ridiculous for her to be dressed up when there was no-one to see her and no-one to entertain.

Now Petula felt that she had an excuse for looking, as Annie would say, "like a proper young lady."

She opened the cupboard door where her mother's gowns were kept and there was the fragrance of roses.

It was the scent her mother had always distilled

herself, and had worn, so whenever the roses came into bloom it was an unforgettable reminder of her.

For a moment Petula shut her eyes and felt the pain of loss within her breasts, which was always there when she thought of her mother and knew how much she missed her.

She took down a gown of pale blue with a white fichu round the shoulders, which had been the fashion five years earlier.

It had a full skirt but Petula did not realise that these were no longer worn. To her it looked beautiful and luxurious.

She laid it on the bed and started to arrange her hair in what she imagined was a fashionable style.

This was difficult because the only guide she had to what was being worn in the world outside Buckden was an occasional copy of *The Ladies Journal* which came her way.

Fortunately, her naturally curly hair looked attractive whatever she did to it, and when she put on her gown Petula knew she looked smarter than she had ever been before!

She only hoped that the Major would appreciate the effort she was making on his behalf, but she thought it unlikely.

There was no time to linger. She had taken far longer to dress than she intended, and with just one last look into the mirror Petula hurried down to the kitchen.

"Have you everything you need, Annie?" she asked.

"I can manage, Miss Petula," Annie replied, "though I'm well aware it's not a large meal for a gentleman as is used to at least half a dozen courses."

"Do you think he really eats half a dozen every night?" Petula asked, curious. "He is very slim, and surely if he devoured as much as that he would be fat."

"Half a dozen is a small dinner in a gentleman's house," Annie said firmly.

She was an authority, Petula knew, because before she had come to work for her mother Annie had been Nursery-maid in a nobleman's household in another part of the County.

It was an enormous house, and ever since she had been tiny Petula had been regaled with stories of how things were done properly by "gentlefolk."

"I've no time to talk now!" Annie said sharply. "I suppose you didn't think to offer the gentleman a glass of wine?"

"Wine?" Petula asked in surprise. "But we have none."

"There's three bottles of your father's claret in the cellar, which I've been hoarding against an emergency," Annie answered. "I've brought a bottle up and opened it, and it should be the right temperature by now."

"Oh, Annie, how splendid of you! I had no idea we had any wine hidden away."

"I wasn't letting just anyone have it, or that Adam, who's always got his tongue hanging out for a drop of liquor," Annie replied. "But I took a peep at our visitor as he walked back from the stables and he's a gentleman if ever I've seen one."

"Yes, he is," Petula agreed. "And I am glad we have the wine, Annie!"

"There's lemonade for you, Miss Petula, and I've got out the extra glasses you'd forgotten."

She pointed with a floury finger to the sideboard.

"How was I to know there was anything with which to fill them?" Petula asked. "Thank you, Annie, you are a marvel!"

She thought as she carried the glasses from the kitchen into the Dining-Room that this was just the sort of situation that Annie enjoyed.

She was in fact an excellent cook, because Petula's mother had trained her, and her father had an appreciation of good food that had made it a challenge to live with him.

If Annie cooked anything he really enjoyed he

21

never forgot to thank her, but she was also well aware when her dishes went wrong and Sir Martin found them unpalatable.

Petula knew that although the food they would have tonight would be simple it would be extremely edible, and she would be surprised if Major Chester, however grand he might appear, did not enjoy it.

Of one thing she was certain, that he would be feeling hungry, and her father had always said that that was a better reason for eating than any other he knew.

It seemed almost like old times to have a man in the house.

As she moved towards the Drawing-Room she thought that what she had missed more than anything else was her father's voice calling her as soon as she came into the house.

She opened the Drawing-Room door.

Her guest was seated in an arm-chair and as she stood for a moment looking at him he rose to his feet, with a smile on his lips.

'This is going to be a very exciting evening,' Petula thought, 'and something I shall remember for the rest of my life!'

Chapter Two

As Petula stared at him wide-eyed she realised that the Major had changed into his evening-clothes.

If she had thought he looked smart before, it was impossible not to gasp at the elgance of his blue long-tailed coat and the skin-tight pantaloons which the Prince of Wales had brought into fashion for informal occasions.

A fob glittered from his waist, but otherwise he wore no jewellery, and the elgance of his skilfully tied snow-white cravat needed no embellishment.

As if the Major realised that she was surprised at his appearance he said,

"I must after all accept your kind offer of hospitality for the night, Miss Buckden. The wheelwright informs me that it is quite impossible for him to complete the work that is required until tomorrow morning."

Petula was unable to find her voice and he went on.

"I hope that neither I nor Jason will be too much of a trouble to you. He is not only my groom but can valet me in emergencies such as this and will also assist your Nurse in the kitchen."

"There is no . . . need for that," Petula murmured.

She felt as if the Major had taken over the house and it was under his command.

She walked across the room, conscious that her mother's gown gave her confidence and feeling that, although she was not sure of it, there was just a touch of admiration in the Major's eyes.

He was in fact as stunned by her appearance as she had been by his.

If she had looked lovely, as she certainly had, in her faded cotton gown with her hair untidy from working in the garden and wearing a sun-bonnet, she was now, he thought, breathtakingly beautiful.

His experienced eye noted that her gown was old-fashioned but it became her, and the white muslin which framed her shoulders revealed the perfection of her skin.

Her hair, also becoming if not skilfully dressed, seemed almost like a golden halo to frame her large eyes and heart-shaped face.

'She is lovely and would be a sensation at St. James's!' the Major said to himself silently.

Then he thought cynically that country flowers did not transplant and it would be a pity to spoil what was perfect in its own environment.

"I hope you have found . . . everything you . . . require," Petula was saying a little breathlessly.

"Jason, like myself, is an old campaigner," the Major replied with a smile, "and what he thinks I need he commandeers in a quite ruthless fashion!"

Petula felt that she should sit down and suggest that her guest do likewise, but at that moment the door opened and Jason announced:

"Dinner is served, Ma'am!"

Petula gave a little laugh as she said:

"It all sounds very grand and I hope you will not be disappointed."

"Shall I say I am beginning to find this a most interesting, not to say exciting, adventure," the Major said. "And infinitely preferable to the large and doubtless dreary dinner-party you envisaged for me."

"It might have been very entertaining," Petula replied as they walked towards the door.

"That is what I think our evening will be together," the Major answered.

She felt herself blushing because there was a note in his voice she had not heard before.

She had arranged the table in the Dining-Room with care, choosing the lace-edged table-cloth which her mother had always kept for best and setting on it the four silver candlesticks which had been in the Buckdens' possession since the reign of George I.

In the centre of them she had set a low bowl filled with syringa and pink rhododendrons, and she had also brought out her mother's best china, which had hardly been used since her death.

She thought with satisfaction that she need not be ashamed of the setting for their dinner and she was sure that Annie would not let her down when it came to the meal.

It was only when she seated herself at the table that she realised she had gone instinctively to her usual chair and had left the head to the Major.

He made no comment but seated himself as if by right in the chair her father had always used.

Then as Jason carried in the first dish Petula realised that Annie was determined to show their guest that she knew how gentry ought to behave.

There was soup to start with from the stock-pot which Annie always kept simmering on the stove, to which had been added, Petula guessed, the mutton-bone and parts of the rabbit which would not be produced later.

It was delicious, and the Major, offered the tureen for the second time, finished everything that was left.

After that there was a spinach soufflé, which had been one of her father's favourites. Petula had found just enough young spinach in the garden for what she thought would be a vegetable for the main course.

"This is exceptionally delicious!" the Major said. "You are fortunate, Miss Buckden, that your Nurse is such a good cook."

"Mama taught her when she first came to us," Petula replied, "and Papa was always very particular about what we ate."

The Major made no further comment, but he ate every piece of the rabbit which Annie had made with a thick sauce to which Petula was certain had been added some of the claret that he was drinking.

The few small plums she had picked from the south wall of the garden were only enough for one person.

So as not to make the Major feel embarrassed at eating alone, she remarked lightly that she did not care for plums and was looking forward to the strawberry season.

He certainly showed no sign of embarrassment when Annie's newly cooked loaf, hot and crisp from the oven, was set in front of him with a small cream cheese and a large pat of butter.

He cut himself a large slice, saying:

"I realise how extremely fortunate I am in not having to put up at the Crown and Feathers."

Jason, who had waited on them silently and with an expertise which Petula felt must have come from long practice, set the decanter of claret on the table and withdrew.

The Major filled his glass, then sat back in his arm-chair very much at his ease and, Petula thought, with an air almost as if he owned the place.

"Now," he said, "let us talk about ourselves."

They had conversed throughout the dinner about horses, the need for the roads of London to be repaired, the vast acres of uncultivated land in Yorkshire, and various other impersonal subjects.

To Petula it had all been very interesting because she had never before dined alone with any man except her father.

"I am afraid there is very little for me to tell you about myself," she answered now, "but I would like to talk about you."

"That, as it happens, is not a subject that interests me at the moment," the Major replied. "I suppose there is no need for me to tell you that you are very beautiful!"

Petula looked at him in astonishment.

Not only had no-one ever told her anything of the sort, but she felt it was a surprising statement from the Major.

He had seemed so condescending when he had first arrived, and had up to this moment made her feel as if nothing was really good enough for him.

She felt the colour rise in her cheeks. At the same time, she knew he was waiting for her answer.

"There is ... really no-one here," she said in a hesitating little voice, "to ... notice what I look like. Adam only admires the vegetables in what he calls 'his garden.'"

She gave a little laugh.

"And the Vicar is ... half-blind. He does not even see when the choir-boys are behaving badly in Church."

"And what is your future to be?" the Major enquired.

Petula made a gesture with her hands.

He noted how graceful they were. Her fingers were long and slim and, despite the fact that she gardened, well kept.

"I cannot ... answer that question," she replied. "I have been expecting to hear from my uncle, but although I have written to him twice I have received no reply."

"You think he will decide what shall happen to you?"

"I really ... do not know," Petula answered. "I have not seen him for many years ... but he is my nearest relative."

"You can hardly live here alone forever," the Major said.

Petula thought he was thinking of the dilapidated house, the holes in the roof of the stable, and the overgrown garden.

Some pride which she did not know she possessed made her lift her chin a little higher.

"This is my home," she said quietly, "and I love it!"

"And you are quite content to stay here, hiding your light under a bushel?" the Major asked. "Then let me tell you again, it is a very lovely light."

"I think you are . . . flattering me," Petula said uncomfortably.

"I am merely telling you the truth."

"I would like to believe you," she answered, "but even if I did, it would not alter my future, which as far as I am concerned is a complete mystery."

"You are beginning to intrigue me."

The Major poured himself another glass of wine and asked:

"What man would not be intrigued? And think what a story it would make!"

He sipped the claret reflectively before he went on:

"I break down in a country lane, find a crumbling old Manor House half in ruins, but in it there is someone so beautiful, so unusually lovely, that she could, if she wished, take London by storm!"

For a moment Petula listened to him spellbound, then she laughed.

"Your story ought to have a happy ending, with a Fairy Godmother waving her wand and transplanting the heroine to London. Alas, that is something which will never happen."

"Can you be sure of that?" the Major enquired.

" 'If wishes were horses, beggars could ride,' " Petula flashed. "But I feel that in London beggar-maids do not arouse much attention."

She had an unselfconsciousness which the Major felt he had never found in any other girl of her age, not that he had conversed with many young women, and he had certainly never dined with one alone.

"Tell me what you think about when you are alone here."

He saw a twinkle in Petula's blue eyes as she replied:

"I spend a lot of time thinking what we shall have to eat. As you saw when you arrived, I have usually to work for my dinner."

"It is doubtless more arduous than singing for it," the Major said. "But when you are not working, what interests you then?"

"Reading, and thank goodness there are a lot of books in the house!"

She smiled as she went on:

"I am sure you would find them very out-of-date, because they were bought by my grandfather, but to me they contain the world in which I cannot travel, the people I shall never have the chance of meeting."

"Suppose we look at your books?" the Major suggested.

"Would you really like to see them?" Petula asked. "I would not like you to sneer at them, at any rate not in their hearing."

"I promise you I am not sneering," he said, "and I will in fact be extremely polite, as I always am, as it happens, towards knowledge of any sort."

"Then come with me," Petula said simply.

He opened the door and she preceded him from the Dining-Room along a passage.

The paint had peeled from the walls and what pictures there were were dark with age.

The furniture had been dusted but there were handles missing from the chests and the chairs had broken legs and wicker seats which had not been repaired.

The Major noticed everything, while to Petula it was too familiar to arouse any comment.

She passed the door into the Drawing-Room where they had sat before dinner and opened a door at the far end of the passage.

It had been, the Major saw at a glance, at one time a magnificent Library, with shelves reaching from the floor to the ceiling, many of them filled with books, but others had large gaps that he felt must once have held leather-bound volumes.

Petula followed the direction of his eyes and said:

"A dealer bought quite a lot of the best books when Papa was ill. He would not give me much for them and I miss them sadly, but they provided the few necessities which the Doctor said Papa must have."

She was not, the Major knew, seeking sympathy but merely stating a fact.

He looked at the books that were left and realised there was a large variety of a type that would interest a scholar more than a young girl.

"Do you really find these interesting?" he asked.

"Absorbingly so," she answered. "Especially the history and the poetry."

The Major did not speak and she went on:

"I cannot tell you how grateful I am to Grandpapa for having a literary taste. Papa, and as far as I can make out most of my ancestors, only cared for horses."

"I thought you liked mine," the Major said.

"I know they are superlative," Petula answered, "but I hardly dare to look at them in case they leave me with no affection for poor old Bessie, who has served us well and faithfully for years."

"Once again you are making yourself out to be a beggar-maid," the Major said. "But let me tell you that your face is your fortune, and with so much wealth I refuse to feel sorry for you."

Petula looked at him mischievously.

"I wonder how much it would fetch in a Sale-Room," she said. "Or do you think a Usurer would advance me a good price for it?"

The Major was just about to make the kind of witty, rather risqué reply which would have been thought extremely amusing in London, but he checked himself.

He knew that Petula spoke in all innocence and again without a touch of self-consciousness.

As if she thought his attention had wandered from the books, she said:

"Shall we go into the Drawing-Room? I think Annie will have made some coffee for you, but I am afraid I cannot offer you a glass of port."

"I am very content with the excellent claret I enjoyed at dinner," the Major said. "I was expecting perhaps another glass of cider."

"That was all I thought I should be able to offer you for dinner," Petula explained, "but Annie always hoardes things away against a rainy day, and you are undoubtedly a tempest!"

The Major laughed and they went into the Drawing-Room.

As she had expected, there was a tray on which stood a small silver teapot which her mother had always used, and two cups and saucers which actually were all that remained of a set that had been broken one by one over the years.

Petula poured out a cup of coffee for the Major, then asked:

"Will you excuse me if I go and speak to Annie and see that she had made up the bed for you?"

"Jason will have already told her we are staying," the Major replied.

"I think I will speak to her too," Petula said.

She went from the Drawing-Room, leaving him alone, and ran upstairs to the room he had used before dinner.

As she had expected, Annie was there pulling back the curtains and turning back the bed, which had already been made up with the best linen sheets.

"The dinner was perfect, Annie!" Petula cried. "And the Major ate everything and really enjoyed it. You really are a genius!"

"You'd have to be a magician to feed a hungry man in this house!" Annie replied uncompromisingly.

At the same time, Petula knew she was pleased at the praise.

"You had something to give his groom?"

"He's had your dinner and mine for tomorrow, so if you go hungry don't blame me!"

"I will not do that," Petula answered. "And it is very exciting to have a visitor!"

Annie made a noncommittal sound, then she said:

"I'll be moving my things for the night into the room next to yours, Miss Petula. I only hope the mattress is not as damp as I expect it to be!"

"Moving into the room next to mine?" Petula asked in astonishment. "But why?"

"I know what's right," Annie replied, "and I'll be waiting up for you, Miss Petula, to make sure you lock your door before you go to bed."

"Lock my door?" Petula repeated. "I cannot think what you are talking about!"

"Then it's time you learnt that young ladies of your age, Miss Petula, are chaperoned," Annie snapped, "and as your poor mother, God rest her soul, can't act in that capacity, I must do my best."

Petula laughed.

"Oh, Annie, you are quite ridiculous! If you are frightened of what people will say about the Major staying here tonight, who's to know except Ben and Adam?"

Annie did not answer and Petula kissed her on the cheek.

"You are an old fuss-pot!" she said. "But you are also a wizard cook. I was so proud of you when each dish was more delicious than the last."

She left the room as she finished speaking, knowing it was impossible to resist the urge to return to the Drawing-Room and be with the Major.

"I may never again have a chance to talk to such a magnificent man," she told herself. "I must not miss a minute of it."

He rose as she came back into the Drawing-

Room, then seated himself in a chair which had its back to the window so that Petula sat opposite him with the evening light on her face.

The sun was setting, and the shadows, like the hills in the distance, were purple and mysterious.

Through the open windows came the shrill, high cries of the bats and the deep "caws" of the rooks going to roost. Otherwise there was a stillness that seemed to have something magical about it.

These were the sounds that Petula heard every night, and her eyes were on the Major's.

She saw that his were grey, steely grey, and she thought there was something penetrating about them, as if he looked deeply into her mind, seeking something, although she had no idea what it was.

Because she felt a little shy she said impulsively:

"Annie has made everything ready for you, and ... you will think it very funny ... she is so afraid of the gossips that she has moved into the room next door to mine and has told me I must lock my door!"

She waited for the Major to laugh, but when he did not she went on:

"I asked her who was likely to talk about my being unchaperoned except Ben, who is only interested in wheels, and Adam, who only wants to talk about potatoes."

"I am glad you are so well looked after," the Major said.

"I told Annie she is an old fuss-pot," Petula remarked, "but she was delighted that you enjoyed your dinner."

She paused before she asked a little anxiously:

"You *did* enjoy it?"

"More than I can tell you," the Major answered, "not only because the food was so good but because I had such an exceptionally interesting companion."

For a moment Petula could not think whom he meant, then she smiled and said:

"Now you are being flattering again. Tell me

33

about the lovely ladies you dine with in London. They
must be very amusing to be with. What do they talk
about?"

"Themselves, and of course—love," the Major answered.

"Love?" Petula questioned, "but . . ."

Her voice died away and after a moment the
Major asked:

"But—what?"

"I was just going to say that you could not want
to talk about love with everybody with whom you
dine. Or perhaps you only dine with . . . one special
person whom you do love?"

The Major smiled secretly at the innocence of the
question, but aloud he said:

"If you think of love in the abstract it is an absorbing subject to most people."

"I never thought of it as . . . being like . . . that,"
Petula said.

"What did you think?"

"I thought that you met somebody," she replied
slowly, "and when you got to know them well you
realised you wanted to be with them for the rest of
your life and they felt the same."

"After that, what do you expect to happen?"

She hesitated and could not look at him, and her
eye-lashes were dark against her cheeks.

"I suppose . . ." she said in a hesitating little voice,
"th-they kiss each other."

"And one should only do that if one is really in
love?" the Major asked.

"Of course," Petula replied. "One could not . . . kiss
anyone . . . otherwise. It would be . . . horrid!"

Again the Major smiled to himself.

"And you think one day that will happen to you?
But if you live here and see no-one except Ben and
Adam, where will your Prince Charming come from?"

"I cannot imagine, although I am sure if fate de-
crees and the gods are propitious he will appear,"

Petula replied lightly. "Perhaps he will have an accident with his Phaeton in the village!"

She spoke teasingly and the Major knew she was not being coquettish or flirtatious as any other woman might have been.

"That is always a possibility," he replied. "Or he may drop down the chimney—like Father Christmas!"

Petula's laughter rang out.

"He would certainly not look very attractive covered in soot! Besides, our chimneys being so old and twisted, he would have to be an acrobat to get down them!"

"That certainly might prove to be an obstacle to true love," the Major said dryly.

"But it would make an exciting story," Petula said. "Oh dear, you are making me feel there are a great many deficiencies after all in my grandfather's Library."

"Shall I suggest instead that you come to London in search of adventure and, of course, the Prince of your dreams?"

For a moment Petula did not answer but looked out the window at the darkening sky.

"I sometimes tell myself a story," she said, "in which I go to London and I do in fact find someone I love, get married, and live happily ever after."

She spoke in a dreamy voice, then her lips curved again in a spontaneous smile.

"Then I remember that I cannot afford the stagecoach even to the next town, let alone London! And it would be a very, very long walk!"

The Major laughed.

"I am afraid you are a pessimist. Most girls of your age, and certainly those who are beautiful, would not be waiting for fate to drop down the chimney or for an accident to happen in the village. They would fight by hook or by crook to get what they wanted."

Not realising she was doing it, Petula rose to her feet and walked towards the window.

"You are making me feel I am foolish and unenterprising," she said. "In fact I am not quite . . . certain what I do . . . want."

The Major had followed her and now stood a little behind her as he said:

"Surely you want what every woman wants? Love and a man to look after you?"

She did not answer, and he said, his voice deepening:

"As I have told you, Petula, you are very beautiful, and there would be a great number of men who would be only too willing to lay their hearts at your feet."

"If I have to go looking for them," Petula replied, "it would spoil the romance. In the story-books the Knight kills the dragon and saves the damsel in distress. She does not go hunting for him!"

That, the Major thought suddenly, was exactly what was wrong with the women he knew in London.

They were all too ready to do their own hunting. In fact they had usually laid out the dragon one way or another long before the Knight appeared.

He was about to speak, but Petula went on:

"I am thinking about what you have said. I shall remember this conversation after you have gone, but I do not feel I have the . . . courage to do the sort of things you suggest, and I am quite sure Mama would not wish me to go to London . . . alone."

"I was not really envisaging your doing so," the Major said.

"Then that makes it very simple," Petula replied. "I shall have to wait until I am asked, and if nobody asks me I must just stay here."

She looked at him with the expression of a child who has just worked out a rather complicated sum.

Then as her eyes met his and it was impossible to look away she felt as if something very strange and inexplicable vibrated between them.

Everything else seemed to fade away except the

36

Major's eyes and there was something magical which linked them like a shaft of moonlight.

How long they remained spellbound Petula afterwards could never calculate, but quite suddenly and unexpectedly the Major said almost harshly:

"I have had a long day, and as I must be up early tomorrow morning I think I would be wise to retire."

For a moment Petula could not find her voice.

Then vaguely, as if she had come back to earth from the heights of a mountain, she replied:

"Yes . . . yes . . . of course . . . Annie will have put a candle in the hall to . . . light you up the . . . stairs."

She would have moved away from the window but the Major was standing just behind her and it was impossible for her to step back into the room until he did so first.

Once again his eyes were on her face.

"When you are older, Petula," he said in a deep voice, "you will realise that I am behaving as your mother and Annie would wish me to do."

Petula looked at him enquiringly and he knew she did not understand.

He took her hand in his.

"Good-night," he said, "and thank you not only for your hospitality but also for showing me there are still things in the world that are unspoilt and as lovely and pure as God intended them to be."

He kissed her hand and she felt his lips against her skin hard, warm, and at the same time strangely compelling.

Then he turned without a word and was gone from the Drawing-Room, closing the door behind him.

She stood where he had left her, conscious only that at his touch something very strange had happened with her breasts.

It was a feeling that she could not understand. She only knew that it left her breathless and tongue-tied and at the same time vibrating as if to music.

She stood still for what might have been a second or an hour. Then as if she remembered her duties she shut the window, latched it, and pulled the curtains.

She moved surefootedly across the darkened room and without the need of a candle went up the stairs and into her bed-room.

She could hear Annie moving about in the next room, and she had just undressed when she opened the door to say:

"Lock your door, Miss Petula, and no arguments about it!"

"Yes, of course, Annie, if you want me to."

It was always easier to do what Annie wished than to try to get her own way.

Annie shut the door and Petula knew she was waiting outside.

She turned the key loudly in the lock and only then did she hear Annie go into the room next door.

Petula got into bed but she could not sleep.

All she could think about was the feeling of the Major's lips against the back of her hand, and after a while she put it on the pillow and laid her cheek against it.

She felt as if it gave her again that strange, unaccountable sensation which seemed to linger in her throat.

"He will be gone tomorrow," she told herself, "but I shall remember forever everything he said to me and how he looked."

She must have fallen asleep, for she awoke to find Annie in the room, pulling back the curtains.

"I had to wake you early, Miss Petula," she said. "With two men in the house and those dratted hens not having laid a single egg!"

Petula sat up in bed to see that Annie was dressed.

"I will go and get some from the farm," she said.

"That's what I thought you'd say," Annie answered. "I'd have sent Adam but he hasn't arrived yet. And he's so slow it'll be luncheon-time before he brings me what I want."

"It will not take me more than ten minutes to cross the field," Petula answered.

She jumped out of bed as she spoke. She washed and dressed herself, and was just about to put on one of her own faded gowns when she hesitated and turned again to the cupboard which contained her mother's things.

Last night the Major had thought her beautiful, and it occurred to her that perhaps this morning he would see that he had been mistaken.

Searching through the cupboard, she chose a pretty gown that her mother had worn only once or twice.

Annie would think it strange, Petula thought, that she should put it on to walk across the field, but she was quite certain that when she got back she would not have time to change before the Major came down to breakfast.

It was still very early and the sun had not properly risen and was only a glow in the east.

The dew was on the grass as Petula hurried across the field holding a wicker basket on her arm.

The home farm where they obtained their milk had once served no-one but the Manor, but it had been let like the other farms on the estate.

The only money that Petula had to live on was the rent paid by the tenant-farmers.

These rents were very small because the farmhouses and other buildings were in such bad repair.

Mrs. Holbridge, the farmer's wife, was a fat and pleasant woman and greeted Petula cheerfully.

"What can I do for ye, Miss Buckden?" she asked. "Ye're surprisingly early."

"We had guests last night," Petula answered. "A gentleman had an accident in the lane and Ben is mending his wheel."

"Then he'll want sommat filling for his breakfast," Mrs. Holbridge said with a smile.

"I would be very grateful if we could have some eggs. Annie used them all up for the dinner last night."

39

"A hungry man'll want more than an egg for his breakfast," Mrs. Holbridge replied. "I'll give ye a cut off our bacon, home-cured."

"That would be very kind of you, Mrs. Holbridge, and of course I will pay you back."

"Ye'll do nothing of th' sort, Miss Buckden!" Mrs. Holbridge replied. "But don't ye go telling Mr. Holbridge or he'll deduct what I be giving ye off th' rent when he pays it. There's none more close-fisted than a Yorkshireman!"

She laughed at her own joke and Petula looked with satisfaction at the large number of brown eggs she was putting into her basket and the slices of bacon, besides several cuts of ham.

"I wish we still had a farm of our own," she said impulsively.

Mrs. Holbridge followed her train of thought.

"Aye, we lives well," she said, "but we works hard for it. Th' men were down in th' fields afore light this morn."

"My father always said what a good farmer Mr. Holbridge was," Petula said politely.

"Your father were a real gentleman, Miss, an' I'm sure ye miss him."

"I do," Petula answered.

She felt Mrs. Holbridge might be about to embark on a long and rambling anecdote about her father that she had heard before, so she quickly took up her basket.

"Thank you, Mrs. Holbridge. You are an angel and I am very, very grateful!" she said, and started back towards the Manor before there could be any further delay.

It had in fact taken her longer than she had expected to reach the farm because the grass had grown higher in the last few weeks and impeded her progress, especially as she was wearing her mother's full-skirted gown.

She therefore walked along the side of the

field where she could move quicker, even though it was a longer way round to the Manor House.

It also meant that unless she was to climb a hedge she must pass through the edge of a small wood before emerging almost directly below the lawn.

It was cool and shadowy under the boughs of the birch trees, and the blue-bells which had made a carpet as blue as her eyes were now fading a little. But there were still primroses vividly yellow against the moss and a number of white violets which Petula told herself she must pick as soon as she had time.

There was a little path winding between the trunks of the trees and she was just reaching the end of it when she saw with a leap of her heart someone coming towards her.

There was no mistaking the Major, and she saw that his polished Hessians were dusty with pollen.

She drew nearer to him and knew that her heart was beating in a peculiar manner, and although she wanted to call out to him naturally, the words would not come to her lips.

"Annie told me where I would find you," he said as they met face to face. "As I was hungry for my breakfast, I thought I might help you to carry it."

"Thank you," Petula said, "but it is not . . . really very . . . heavy."

She wondered why her voice sounded so strange, then once again as she looked up at the Major it was impossible to look away.

"I also wanted to say good-bye to you," he said, "which is something I omitted to do last night."

Petula thought that his voice sounded strange. But she could think of nothing except his eyes looking deep into her heart.

The Major took the basket from her arm and set it down on the ground; then, while she waited, feeling as if she were in a dream, he put his arms round her.

"I could not sleep for thinking about you," he said, and then his lips were on hers.

For a moment Petula could only feel surprise that this should be happening.

Then the sensations she had felt in her breasts when he had kissed her hand were there again, only intensified until she felt the wonder of them invade her whole body like a streak of sunlight.

The Major's lips were at first hard against the softness and innocence of hers, then they were so tender and gentle that she felt as if her whole being reached out to become a part of him.

It was so wonderful, so perfect, that Petula felt as if they were alone in a secret place far removed from the world—a place of magic and indescribable beauty—and knew a glory that was part of God.

The Major held her captive and she thought that her soul passed into his keeping before he said in a voice that was curiously unsteady:

"That is the right ending to a fairy-story."

Petula could not move, she could only look up at him, her eyes filling her whole face, telling him without words what she felt.

She thought he would kiss her again, but he said abruptly:

"We must go back. I have to be on my way as soon as possible!"

Chapter Three

The Phaeton disappeared out of sight at the turn of the drive and Petula stood for a long time looking at the place where she had last seen it.

Then a sigh seemed to come from the very depths of her being.

This, as the Major had said, was the end of the dream.

They had walked back to the house in silence, until as they stood on the unkept lawn he turned to look at her face with an expression in his eyes which she could not fathom.

"This has been a dream," he said quietly, "an enchantment which I think neither of us will forget."

He paused for a moment and then went on:

"We will not meet again, Petula, but never will I find elsewhere such a perfect moment of magic."

He had not touched her, but she felt from the deep note in his voice that he held her in his arms.

As if he forced himself to do so he walked on into the house through the open windows of the Drawing-Room.

She had known that he did not want her to follow him, so she took her basket round to the kitchen entrance.

Annie was fussing and fuming in the kitchen.

"How could you have been so long?" she asked. "The gentleman is up and wanting to be on his way."

Petula did not reply. She only went up to her room to stare at her face in the mirror as if she felt it must have completely changed.

She could still feel the impression of the Major's lips on hers, still feel his heart beating against her breasts as he held her close against him.

It was as if she walked in a dream; but the dream was coming to an end and she would wake to find reality.

She was aware at the back of her mind, although somehow she could not bring herself to think clearly, that the Major was having his breakfast and that Jason had brought the Phaeton round to the front door.

Then at the very last minute when the Major was picking up his high-crowned hat in the hall, she walked down the stairs.

Knowing instinctively that she was there, he raised his eyes to watch her coming slowly down with the grace that he had noticed the first time they had walked from the garden to the house.

She held her chin high, but her eyes were large and dark in her small face.

When she reached the hall she stood looking up at the Major and it seemed as if again they both were spellbound.

"Good-bye, Petula," he said, and his voice, although low, seemed to vibrate round the small hall.

"Good-bye," she replied, and the words were hardly above a whisper.

For a long, long moment they looked into each other's eyes. Then one of the horses outside the door shook its bridle and broke the spell.

Without another word, without touching Petula's hand, the Major walked down the steps and climbed into the Phaeton.

Hardly aware that her feet were moving, Petula followed to stand watching the horses move away, noting with one part of her mind the expert manner in which the Major handled them.

Jason raised his hat but the Major looked ahead, his lips set in a tight line, his chin very square.

The Phaeton lurched over the holes in the drive, but it was only a question of seconds before the horses, fresh and eager to be on their way, had reached the turn. Then they were out of sight.

"I shall never see him again," Petula murmured beneath her breath.

She waited for the pain to strike her almost as if she drove a dagger into her own breast.

Still feeling as if she was not really awake, she walked across the hall as Annie came hurrying down the passage from the kitchen.

"Miss Petula, what do you think?" she cried.

Not waiting for Petula to answer, she went on:

"The gentleman's groom pressed something into m' hand when he said good-bye and told me that he and his master had spent a comfortable night. Most grateful they were for the hospitality we gave them."

She opened her hand as she spoke and stared at what it contained before she went on:

"I didn't look at what he'd given me until now, but see what it is, Miss Petula!"

With an effort Petula forced herself to look at what Annie held in her hand.

There were two large gold coins, each, she knew, worth five guineas!

"Ten guineas, Miss Petula!" Annie said in awe-struck tones. "Ten guineas for one night! I can hardly believe what I sees with me own eyes!"

"You . . . you gave them a very g-good dinner," Petula said in a voice that did not sound like her own.

"Well, we'll certainly not go hungry this week!" Annie exclaimed. "I told you he was a real gentleman and there's no mistake about that!"

"No, Annie, there is . . . no mistake about that," Petula agreed, and walked into the Drawing-Room.

There were a dozen things she ought to be doing and she was sure that Adam was expecting her in the garden.

But all she could think of was the elegance of the Major when they had talked here and the feeling that she had had when she had stood at the window with him just behind her.

Now she knew, although she had not realised it at the time, that she wanted him to kiss her and that he must have felt the same. She knew now that that was what he had meant when he said:

"When you are older, Petula, you will realise that I am behaving as your mother and Annie would wish me to do."

If he had only kissed her then, she thought, she would have not only one enchanted moment to remember, but two.

"I must go back to the wood," she told herself.

She wanted to hold on to the wonder and glory that had happened there before she lost it as she had lost the Major.

She walked out through the window to the lawn, but she had not gone more than a few yards when she heard Annie's voice.

"Where are you a-going, Miss Petula? I wants you to help me make up the bed."

Petula turned round.

Annie was speaking to her from the window of the room which had been her father's, where the Major had spent the night.

"Can it not wait?" she asked.

"I want to do it now, before I goes to the village," Annie replied.

Reluctantly Petula retraced her steps into the house and walked up the stairs.

Annie had already stripped the linen sheets from the big four-poster and was opening out another pair which she had taken from the linen cupboard.

"Come along, Miss Petula," she said sharply. "It's unlike you to be dawdling about the place. I was thinking we could have a nice bit of beef for luncheon. We can certainly afford it this week."

She threw a sheet across the bed and Petula automatically began to open it.

It smelt of lavender because her mother had always insisted that fresh bags of lavender be made every year for the linen cupboard at the same time that she made pot-pourri.

"I do not know why we are making up this bed again," Petula remarked. "The Major will . . . not be coming . . . back."

There was a little throb in her voice as she spoke the last words, but Annie did not notice.

"I've a feeling in my bones," she answered, "that, having had one visitor, we might have another."

"That is most unlikely!" Petula replied, thinking there would not be another accident in the village for perhaps twenty years.

"Have you forgotten we're still expecting your uncle?"

"He did not answer my first letter," Petula answered, "so there is no reason to expect that he will reply to my second."

"One never knows," Annie replied. "Postmen are none too reliable, and we're a long way from London."

Then as they covered the top sheet with the blankets Annie said in a different voice:

"I was just thinking, Miss Petula, that it'd be unwise for you to tell anybody, especially your uncle, if he ever does arrive, that the gentleman stayed here last night."

Petula looked at her and Annie went on:

"You know as well as I do that people have nasty minds and even longer tongues. I looked after you as your mother would have wished, but who would believe the word of a servant?"

She spoke without bitterness and continued:

"Now you be a sensible girl and do as I say. Just forget that we had a visitor, though it's grateful enough we are for what he left behind."

As if she suddenly realised that Petula was unresponsive, she said:

"Promise me, dearie! I know what's best and you can trust me to decide what's right."

"I do trust you, Annie," Petula replied, "and of course I promise, if it will make you happy."

"That's my girl!" Annie said, and smiled approvingly.

She picked up the velvet cover and she and Petula spread it over the bed.

"I'll brush the floor and draw the curtains again when I come back," Annie said. "And now I'll get my bonnet and cape. Luncheon'll be a bit late, but it'll be well worth waiting for!"

She bustled away down the passage and Petula stood there for a moment, thinking that this was where the Major had slept last night.

His head had touched the pillows. He had seen himself reflected in the walnut-framed mirror which stood over the inlaid chest-of-drawers which her father had always used as a dressing-table.

She went to the window.

Across the field she could see the spring green of the trees in the wood.

As if afraid that she would once again be stopped, she ran down the stairs and out through the Drawing-Room window, and crossed the lawn as swiftly as her feet could carry her.

* * *

Luncheon was not finished until two o'clock, but Annie had enjoyed the beef she had brought back from the village and the excellent local cheese with which they completed the meal.

It had been difficult for Petula to force herself to eat anything. She felt as if every mouthful stuck in her throat and it was an effort to swallow it.

But she knew how disappointed Annie would be, so she forced herself to look as though she were eating a lot.

When Annie left the room to fetch something from the kitchen she placed the slices of beef on her place back onto the dish beside the joint, hoping that Annie would not notice.

"Let's hope," Annie said as she cleared away, "that you'll put on a little weight in the next week or so. I'm sick and tired of taking in your gowns round the waist, and the best present you could give me would be the need to let them out again."

"I am no thinner than Mama was," Petula answered. "Her gown last night fitted me well."

"Your mother was nothing but skin and bone the last years of her life," Annie answered, "waiting hand and foot on your father and worrying about him, and you. She was like a sylph, as I always told her."

Petula smiled.

"You would like me to be as plump as a German Frau, Annie, and that I have no intention of ever being."

As she spoke she opened the Dining-Room door to carry the plates into the kitchen.

Even when they were alone Annie would never allow her to eat anywhere but in the Dining-Room.

"I knows what's right, Miss Petula," she often said. "I'm not having you sitting down in my kitchen, which isn't your rightful place, as you're well aware!"

It made a lot of extra work and a lot of walking about, Petula thought.

But she knew that Annie was trying to preserve some semblance of gentlefolk's behaviour despite the fact that they lived in a house that was crumbling about their ears and possessed hardly enough money to keep themselves alive.

As she reached the passage she stopped.

"What is it?" Annie asked, who was just behind her.

"I think it is someone at the front door."

Petula put the plates she was carrying down on a table in the passage and walked towards the hall.

The door had been left open after the Major had

departed, and now to her astonishment she saw through the open doorway a vehicle standing outside.

For one moment her heart missed a beat as she thought that the Major had returned. Then she realised it was not a Phaeton she saw but a post-chaise drawn by two horses.

Already in the hall, standing some way from the door so that she had not noticed him at first, was a gentleman.

She glanced at him and realised, although she had not seen him for ten years, that it was her uncle.

There was indeed a resemblance to her father, but Roderick Buckden, more slender and dressed in the height of fashion, was far more elegant than her father had ever managed to be.

"You must be Petula!" he exclaimed.

"Uncle Roderick ... you have come at last!" Petula cried. "I thought you could not have received my letters."

"I received a letter from you a little over three weeks ago," he replied, "in which you referred to one you had written earlier. That one never reached me."

"I sent it to the only address that Papa had for you," Petula explained. "Then, as you did not reply, I thought I should write again, and remembered that your Club was St. James's."

"It is one of my Clubs," her uncle answered. "But you must have written to an old address. That is the explanation why I did not come at once, and I had no idea that your father was dead."

"He died just before Christmas."

"I am sorry. I should have been here for the funeral."

Her uncle spoke vaguely, and Petula realised that he was looking round the hall: at the panes of glass that were missing in the long windows on either side of the front door; at the paper peeling from the walls above the pictures, which were dark with age; and at the stair-carpet, which was so threadbare that it was hard to know what colour it had been originally.

"The place looks much shabbier than I remember it," he remarked.

"I am . . . afraid so, Uncle Roderick," Petula replied, "but there has been no money to spend on repairs or redecoration. Papa was very ill before he . . . died. I suggested writing to tell you so, but he did not wish to be a trouble to anybody."

Her uncle's face seemed to soften a little. She thought he had a hard expression, and his eyes were certainly disapproving of what they saw, although she could not blame him for that.

"I presume," he said, "that what you are implying is that there is little of value left in the house?"

"I have sold only a . . . few things," Petula said apologetically, "to provide Papa with medicines which the Doctor ordered and the food he said was essential."

"So, I am the Beggar Baronet."

"You have naturally inherited the title, as Papa had no . . . son."

Her uncle looked at her face for the first time.

"Well, he certainly had a very pretty daughter," he said. "You had better tell me what else is left, but first I must pay the post-chaise."

As he spoke, his driver, a rather surly-looking man in an ill-fitting coat carried in two valises which he set down just inside the front door.

" 'Ere ye are, Gov'nor," he said, "and if ye've no further use for me services I'll be on me way."

Petula saw her uncle draw three sovereigns from his pocket.

The driver took them, stared at them disdainfully, and said:

"That don't leave me much fe meself."

"You have had what is your due," Sir Roderick replied, "and those last horses were not worth hiring."

"Ye're lucky to find an animal with four legs in this benighted part of the world," the driver retorted.

He put the sovereigns in his pocket and walked away as he spoke, without raising his cap.

"Impertinent fellow!" Sir Roderick remarked to Petula. "But at least I have managed to get here, although damned expensive it has proved to be!"

"I am sorry, Uncle Roderick," Petula said, as if he accused her of it being her fault.

"The house appears to be in a rotten state," Sir Roderick said, walking towards the Drawing-Room.

"The top floor is uninhabitable," Petula answered. "And Annie and I have shut the rooms we are not using, but I am afraid a number of the ceilings have fallen."

Sir Roderick looked round the Drawing-Room as if he was appraising everything in it and was disgusted with what he saw. He sat down in a chair.

"Have you had luncheon?" Petula asked politely.

"Yes, I called at a Posting Inn two hours ago," her uncle replied, "but I would like a drink—if there is anything left in the cellar."

"There are, I believe, two bottles of Papa's claret," Petula answered.

She remembered as she spoke how the Major had enjoyed one last night.

"Well, that is better than nothing!" Sir Roderick said.

"Shall I fetch it for you?" Petula enquired.

"In a moment," he said. "Let me look at you. I thought when I was last here—was it nine or ten years ago?—you were a pretty little thing. Now, dammit, you have grown into a beauty!"

"I am glad you approve of me, Uncle Roderick," Petula said, "because you are my only relative left."

"I suppose that is true," Sir Roderick agreed reflectively. "But what about your mother's side of the family?"

"You know Mama's family lived right in the North of Scotland, and most of them I think are dead. Anyway, they gave up writing to her a long time ago."

"Then there are only you and I to represent the Buckdens," Sir Roderick said, "but it does not appear as if we have much to represent!"

"Are you going to live here, Uncle Roderick?"

"Live here!" he exclaimed. "Good God, no! What I am wondering is if there is any fool who is likely to buy it from me."

"Buy it?"

Petula could not have been more surprised if he had exploded a bomb under her feet.

"B-but ... Uncle Roderick," she expostulated, "it has been in the family for five hundred years!"

"Who cares if it is five thousand?" her uncle replied. "What I want, Petula, is not this dilapidated ruin in the middle of nowhere, but some money."

"That is something we certainly do not have."

"How many acres?" he enquired.

"Just over seven hundred. The three farms are let, but they pay us very little rent because the houses and out-buildings are in such bad repair."

Her uncle's lips tightened and she said tentatively:

"There was a man here about six months ago ... just before Papa ... died, who asked me if the ... house was for ... sale."

"Who was he? Did you get his name?"

"Yes, he was a man called Barrowick, and I think he is very rich. He has a factory about thirty miles away, and Annie thought that he had pretensions of being 'Lord of the Manor'!"

" 'Pretensions' is the right word!" her uncle replied. "You say he is rich?"

"That is what Annie was told in the village, but I only spoke to him for a few minutes."

"And you said the house was not for sale?"

"Of course," Petula answered. "I had no idea you would ever think of ... disposing of what has always been an ... heirloom handed down from ... father to son."

"Well, I certainly cannot afford an heir," her uncle said, "so the sooner this encumbrance is off my hands the better!"

"B-but ... Uncle Roderick ..." Petula began.

Then she thought that anything she might say would be a waste of her breath.

She could understand in a way what her uncle felt.

At the same time, it seemed wrong that he should be so anxious to be rid of the Manor, even though she knew it would cost hundreds if not thousands of pounds to restore it to its original state.

Her uncle had risen to walk to the window.

"Seven hundred acres," he said reflectively, "the house—and I suppose there are a few cottages?"

"Twelve," Petula said automatically.

Her uncle did not speak and she knew that as he was looking out over the fields he was calculating exactly what he could get from Mr. Barrowick if he was still an interested purchaser.

She drew in her breath.

"If you . . . sell the Manor, Uncle Roderick," she asked in a nervous little voice, "what is to . . . become of me?"

Her uncle did not answer for a moment. Then he said:

"Come here, Petula!"

Obediently she went to his side and he half-turned from the window to look at her.

The sun on her face revealed the clearness of her skin and the vivid blue of her eyes, and turned her hair to shining gold.

"I have an idea," he said slowly.

"An idea, Uncle Roderick?"

"No, dammit!" he exclaimed. "It is more than an idea—it is an inspiration!"

"What is?"

His eyes left her face and she knew that he was looking at her figure, appraising her, she thought, almost as if she were a horse.

"Do you know what I am, Petula?" he asked.

"What you are, Uncle Roderick? I do not understand."

"Then let me tell you," he said. "I am a gambler. I have always been a gambler—not because it amuses me, not because I am obsessed as so many Rakes are by the turn of a card, but simply because I have to live."

Petula stared at him wide-eyed as he went on:

"It is the only way that I can enjoy the company of my fellow men in the Social World, which amuses me."

"But ... what happens if you ... lose?" Petula asked.

Her uncle smiled.

"Then I am in the uncomfortable position in which I find myself at this moment—owing more than I possess."

"You mean ... you are in debt?"

"Exactly!"

"So that is why you will have to sell the Manor."

"There is no alternative," he said. "At the same time, although that may solve my problems for the moment, there still remains a question mark over the future."

"You mean you may easily be in the same ... position again once the ... money has ... run out?"

"Very easily."

Petula waited; at the same time, she began to feel afraid.

It did not seem as if her uncle would give her and Annie anything to live on, in which case what would become of them?

"I told you I am a gambler," her uncle said slowly, "and when one gambles, Petula, one develops an instinctive sense."

"I do not ... understand," she said quickly. "Please explain to me."

"It is difficult to put into words," her uncle replied, "but sometimes I know before the turn of a card what it will be; sometimes a feeling I cannot explain saves me at the very last moment from disaster."

He spoke in a strange tone, almost, Petula thought, as if he was seeing clairvoyantly what might happen; then he said:

"Now I have this feeling about you."

55

"A-about me . . . Uncle Roderick?"

"I know that you are the right card for me to play at this precise moment."

Petula waited. She did not wish to say again that she did not understand.

"What we are going to do," Sir Roderick said, "is to return to London as Sir Roderick Buckden with his beautiful niece, who is a great Yorkshire heiress."

Petula stared at her uncle as if she thought he had taken leave of his senses.

"An . . . heiress?" she repeated, thinking she could not have heard him aright.

"An heiress!" he said firmly. "Beauty is important in the world in which I live, Petula, but not as important as money."

"B-but . . . but we have no . . . money!"

"We shall have what I get from the sale of the estate."

"You know it will not be much."

"Yes, I know that and you know that," Sir Roderick said, "but nobody else will know it."

"I still do not . . . understand."

"Let me put it very clearly. You, my very attractive niece, are going to find yourself a rich husband. As soon as you are married, you will pay me half of everything your husband gives you, and with your looks it ought to be a very considerable sum."

Petula was speechless. She could only stare at him.

"You can leave the Marriage Settlement and all other financial problems to me," Sir Roderick said airily. "All you have to do is to captivate one of the rich men to whom I shall introduce you, and you can believe me when I tell you that I know a great many."

"W-why . . . should they wish to . . . marry me?"

Sir Roderick smiled as if the question was so childish that it was hardly worth a reply, then he said:

"A beautiful woman, young and unspoilt, is quite a rarity in London at this moment, but beauty is considerably enhanced by a golden halo. That, my dear, is what everyone will believe you have."

"But . . . it is . . . untrue!"

"As I have already said, nobody else will know that."

"But . . . Uncle Roderick, I do not think I am . . . capable of . . . acting such a . . . lie, pretending that I am . . . rich when I have . . . nothing."

Petula spoke hesitantly and was conscious that her uncle's eyes narrowed.

"Of course, if you can keep yourself adequately without my assistance, you can always refuse my offer."

"You know I . . . cannot do . . . that," Petula said in a low voice.

"Then stop arguing and leave everything to me," her uncle said. "Go and fetch that bottle of claret you were talking about, and then I would like to see the Estate Accounts, if you keep them."

"Yes, I keep them," Petula answered.

She went from the room to fetch the bottle of claret which Annie had hidden away in the cellar against a "rainy day."

When she brought it back into the Drawing-Room a little while later she felt as if her mind could not take in what her uncle had said.

It seemed impossible that he should mean her to act a part for which she felt she was fundamentally unsuited and which would be a lie intended to deceive someone who would obviously trust them.

"I cannot do such a thing," Petula told herself. "Papa would not approve of it, and Mama would be . . . horrified!"

But, she asked herself, what was the alternative?

She was afraid of the answer even as it formed in her mind.

* * *

After some difficulty in finding a vehicle to convey him to Huntry, where Mr. Barrowick had his fac-

Barbara Cartland

tory, Sir Roderick left the Manor at about ten o'clock the following morning.

He had no sooner driven away than Petula ran into her father's Library and took out his Will from a drawer in the desk.

Her uncle had asked for it last night and she had told him that she had mislaid it but would find it by the time he returned.

"I do not suppose it is worth the paper it is written on," he said, "but I might as well see it."

"I think, Uncle Roderick, Papa thought that ... you would look ... after me."

"And that is exactly what I intend to do," her uncle said.

He talked to Petula until late in the evening and everything he said made her feel more and more afraid.

What had horrified her more than anything else was when she asked, a little tentatively because she almost anticipated the answer:

"Will I be able to bring ... Annie with me to London?"

"Certainly not!" her uncle had replied. "To begin with I cannot afford it, and secondly your lady's-maid must be well trained in the arranging of your hair in a fashionable manner and used to looking after expensive gowns."

"What ... will happen to A-Annie?" Petula asked almost piteously. "Papa would have given her a pension."

"What with?" her uncle asked almost brutally.

After they had gone to bed Petula had lain awake, not thinking about herself but about Annie.

How could she abandon her old Nurse penniless and at her age unlikely to get other employment?

Then, just as her uncle had had an inspiration, she had one too.

Now she drew out her father's Will and added a codicil to it.

It was not difficult to copy her father's writing, and Petula inscribed on the heavy parchment:

> *To Annie Bacon, who has been in my em-*
> *ployment for so many years I leave for her*
> *lifetime Honeysuckle Cottage, and to Adam*
> *Ives also for his lifetime No. 1 Church Cot-*
> *tage, both on my estate in the village of*
> *Buckden.*

Petula signed her father's name at the bottom of the codicil, copying it exactly from the signature above it. Then, carrying the Will in her hand, she went into the kitchen.

"I have just realised, Annie," she said, "that when you witnessed Papa's Will you omitted to add your signature to the codicil. For it to be legal you should have signed twice."

"Surely it is too late now?" Annie asked.

"Of course it is not!" Petula answered. "You were there when Papa signed his Will and you verified his signature."

"Yes, of course," Annie agreed.

Petula put a pen in her hand.

"Sign here, Annie," she said.

The old maid obeyed her, scrawling her name rather laboriously.

The other witness to her father's signature had been the Doctor. He, however, had left the village soon after her father's death to take up a more lucrative post in Richmond.

His signature was a little difficult to copy, but Petula managed it.

Then she left the Will on the desk, ready for her uncle's return, and hurried back to the kitchen.

"Now listen to me, Annie," she said. "This is important, so please stop whatever you are doing."

"I suppose you want some luncheon," Annie retorted.

"That is quite immaterial compared with what we have to do now."

Petula spoke in a voice which made Annie look at her in surprise.

"My uncle is taking me with him to London," she said, "but he is making no provision either for you or for Adam."

She saw Annie's cheeks pale, and she added quickly:

"But Papa remembered you. He left Honeysuckle Cottage, Annie, which as you know is empty at the moment since old Mrs. Burton died three months ago."

"Honeysuckle Cottage!" Annie said. "Well, that was real kind of your father, Miss Petula, but I never thought as I'd be leaving you."

"I do not wish to leave you, Annie, but I have to do what Uncle Roderick wishes."

"I understand," Annie said, but Petula knew she was upset.

"We will talk about that later," she said quickly. "What we have to do at this moment is to furnish Honeysuckle Cottage."

"Furnish it? What do you mean, Miss Petula?"

"Uncle Roderick has gone to Huntry to sell the estate to that man who called when Papa was ill. He intends to sell everything, as he put it, 'Lock, stock and barrel.'"

"Then what are you saying, Miss Petula?"

"I am saying that you are going to have the things which are really mine—the furniture which belonged to Mama, and all the little things she loved and I love too because they belonged to her."

"What will your uncle say?"

"He will not know," Petula answered. "He has not even bothered since he arrived to go round the house. How could he be aware of what is in my bed-room, where we put so many of Mama's treasures, or of what is left in the other rooms?"

She saw that Annie understood what she was saying, and she turned towards the door.

"I am sending Adam to the farm to borrow Ned and the wagon, and you and I will get what we can down into the hall."

Afterwards Petula thought that only by being so authoritative, and, as Annie said, "by taking her breath away from her," was she able to get her own way.

Fortunately, they both knew Honeysuckle Cottage well, and as it happened it was about the only cottage on the estate that was not in a very bad state of repair.

Old Mrs. Burton, who had died there, had been a widow with a certain amount of money of her own.

She had therefore not relied on Sir Martin to repair and redecorate the small cottage she rented from him but had paid for the work herself.

She had even added on to the original cottage, which meant there were two bed-rooms, a pleasant Sitting-Room, and a small Dining-Room opening out of the kitchen.

All day until it was dark Petula and Annie carried things down the stairs and filled up the wagon, with the help of Adam and Ned.

Then, sitting in the front of it, they drove to Honeysuckle Cottage and arranged everything in the small rooms.

Petula insisted on taking the best carpets, the rugs that were not too worn, and choosing the prettiest and least faded curtains for the windows.

"I can't be taking all this, Miss Petula," Annie said a dozen times.

"Do you wish Mr. Barrowick to have it all?" Petula would ask angrily. "And what will he do with it? Put it on the bonfire, I should not wonder."

Annie was silenced and they went on working.

They were both exhausted by the time they went to bed, but Petula was up again at five-thirty, driving Annie to bring down more things.

There were mirrors from her mother's room that she felt were of no great value but she had known them since she was a child.

There was linen from the cupboard on the stairs, and she even found a small, disused canteen of silver which was not marked with the Buckden crest and which she insisted on Annie having.

"You are taking them for me as well as yourself," she said to every protest the old woman made.

By noon Honeysuckle Cottage seemed crammed from floor to ceiling.

Petula then told Adam that his cottage was his for life and that he was to take every tool he was likely to require to work his own garden and perhaps to go out jobbing in the village.

Adam did not argue.

He filled his wheel-barrow with forks, spades, hoes, trowels, and watering-cans, and trundled them down the twisting path through the shrubberies, which was the quickest way to his small cottage, which stood next to the Church-yard.

When Petula got back to the Manor she said to Annie:

"Now we have to think how you are going to live."

"I'll manage somehow, dearie," Annie said in a tired voice.

"You have to manage only until I can send you some money from London," Petula said, "and I promise you I shall not forget to do that. But first of all, have you something left from what the Major gave you?"

"Something left?" Annie replied. "I should think I have, Miss Petula! I'm not throwing good money away."

"Then keep it carefully and do not mention to my uncle that you have anything," Petula told her. "I am going to ask him to pay the bills we owe in the village before we leave, and I think he can hardly refuse me."

"There's something about him, smart though he appears, that makes me worry for you," Annie said slowly.

Petula thought that if Annie knew the truth she would worry a great deal more, but because she knew there was nothing the old maid could do she merely replied:

"Do not worry about me, Annie, I am worrying about you. I am going now to the farm."

"What for?"

"The rent is due on the thirty-first of March, as we all know, but Mr. Holbridge is always late, just as the others are. I am going to collect it."

"What you get from the tenants belongs to your uncle," Annie said.

"Perhaps he will forget about it," Petula replied, and hurried off to the farm.

When Sir Roderick returned an hour before dinner-time and swept through the front door, Petula knew that he had succeeded in what he had set out to do.

There was an expression of elation on his face that she had not seen before as he put his arm round her shoulders and said:

"I have good news for you, my dear, very good news!"

"You have sold the Manor and the estate?" Petula asked in a small voice.

"I have sold it—and sold it very well!" he answered. "Barrowick was dead keen, as you suspected, to become the Lord of the Manor. He had to pay through the nose for the privilege, but he can well afford it!"

"I am glad you are ... pleased, Uncle Roderick."

"You can be pleased too," her uncle answered. "Now we can do things in style, and that is the right word, Petula!"

He looked at her in an appraising manner as he flung himself down on a chair in the Drawing-Room.

"You will pay for dressing, and I do not mind betting that in a few weeks after you reach London you will be the toast of Saint James's."

Petula clasped her hands together.

"L-listen . . . Uncle Roderick," she said. "Now that you have the money you want, why not leave me a little . . . a very . . . little of it, and let me . . . stay here in Yorkshire. I shall be quite . . . happy with Annie in the cottage which Papa left her in his . . . Will."

"Left her a cottage?" Sir Roderick asked sharply. "You did not tell me that."

"I hardly realised it myself until I read Papa's Will. Shall I fetch it for you?"

"Yes, let me have a look at it," her uncle said.

Petula, with her heart beating apprehensively, fetched the Will from the Library.

She put it into Sir Roderick's hands and was silent while he read it.

"I see it is only for her lifetime," he said at length, "and the same applies to the man Adam. That will not alter the deal I have made with Barrowick."

"And what about my . . . staying with Annie?"

"Can you be so childish and so utterly insane as to wish to bury yourself here, looking like you do?" her uncle asked. "My dear girl, I am going to put the world at your feet! The world of the Bucks and the Beaux, the world which centres round the Prince of Wales, who is the biggest Beau of them all!"

"I . . . I really do not want . . . that," Petula said, and realised even as she spoke that her uncle was not listening to her.

"I promised to give you a halo of gold," he said, with a smile on his lips, "and that is exactly what you are going to have. Who is going to guess for one moment that it is fairy-gold which cannot be touched by human hands?"

He laughed, and as he did so Petula shivered.

Chapter Four

"You were a great success last night, dear," the Honourable Mrs. Warren said to Petula in her gentle voice.

Petula smiled and was about to reply when her uncle said sharply:

"What did Lord Crowhurst say to you?"

"He paid me a lot of silly compliments," she answered lightly.

Then as she saw her uncle frown she realised that she had said the wrong thing.

"Crowhurst is a very rich man!" he retorted.

Petula wanted to add that he was also old, ugly, and frightening.

But she had learnt by this time that it was a mistake to criticise and her uncle expected her to be amenable and submissive to everything he suggested.

She had in fact felt, since she had left Yorkshire, as if she were being swept along by a typhoon which left her breathless and at times unable to think clearly.

To begin with, everything was new and bewildering, and although there was a great deal that was exciting there were also a great many things which made her afraid.

They had arrived in London and Sir Roderick had taken her to a small house in Islington which belonged, Petula found, to the Honourable Mrs. Warren.

Petula had learnt on her way down from the North that she was to be her chaperon. She was a sweet-faced woman nearing middle-age and Petula had taken to her immediately.

"Mrs. Warren," her uncle explained, "belongs to one of the oldest families in England, and her brother-in-law is Lord Warrencliff, a Gentleman-in-Waiting to the King."

It did not take Petula long to discover that Mrs. Warren was prepared to do anything her uncle asked because she was in love with him.

She also learnt, though it took a little time to discover all the details, that Mrs. Warren's hope and prayer was one day to be married to Sir Roderick.

Unfortunately, she had no money except what her husband had left her on his death.

This was enough to keep her in comparative comfort, but if she married again it would be taken from her as would the house in which she lived.

As they neared London Petula had said to her uncle:

"This lady who is to chaperon me . . . are you going to inform her that I am an heiress or will you tell her the . . . truth?"

"No-one—and I mean no-one—is to know anything except what I tell them about you," her uncle said positively.

He thought out more of the story and Petula learnt that she had only just come into so much wealth, which had been left to her by a relative on her mother's side who had made a great fortune in the West Indies.

"You do not have the handling of the capital," her uncle said, and she knew he was inventing as he went along, "until you are twenty-five or *you get married.*"

He said the last three words with an impressive note in his voice which told Petula that this was the key to the whole masquerade.

"U-Uncle Roderick," she said in a worried tone, "what I do not . . . understand is, if I have such a large fortune, why should anyone rich wish to marry me? Surely it would be a poor man who would find me desirable?"

"You leave the poor men to me," her uncle said grimly. "I am used to impecunious fortune-hunters. I can recognise them a mile off."

"But the rich men have their own money," Petula persisted.

Her uncle smiled cynically.

"No man is so rich that he does not wish for more, and, what is more important, he wants to be married for himself, not for what he possesses."

He smiled.

"It will be your job, Petula, to convince someone with money that it is of no consequence and that you love him as a man."

"B-but if I do not . . . love him?"

"Then you will pretend to!" her uncle shouted at her. "You have to act a part, Petula! Good God, every woman can act if she wants to!"

He looked at her frightened eyes and added in a gentler tone:

"It will not be too difficult for you, for as your Guardian I shall make it very hard for a man to be alone with you."

He let Petula absorb this before he added:

"Traditionally, heiresses are kept strictly in their golden cages and no-one can open the door unless they can provide the key—which is a wedding-ring."

He laughed at his own fantasy, then went on:

"Leave everything to me, Petula. I realise that you are young and inexperienced, but that is at least ninety per cent of your charm. London men are satiated with sophisticated beauties who fall into their arms almost before they ask them to do so."

He looked her over in the calculating manner she disliked before he said:

"You will be the unobtainable—or almost—and that will prove a challenge."

Petula felt that she had no wish to be anything of the sort, but she told herself she was being extremely ungrateful, especially as her uncle was being so generous as regards clothes.

The day after they arrived, the dressmakers came flooding into the small house in Islington, bringing with them sketches, patterns, and even models of the gowns they had to sell.

Everything they suggested was carefully scrutinised and appraised by Sir Roderick.

Petula's opinion was not asked and she realised that he and Mrs. Warren were experts and the results of their choices were certainly inexpressibly lovely.

When they attended the first Reception to which they had been invited, Petula found that she was in fact the success which her uncle had envisaged.

How much was due to her appearance and how much to the stories that were already in circulation about her fortune was debatable.

The first thing Sir Roderick had done on arrival was to send a notice to the *Gazette* saying:

Sir Roderick Buckden, Baronet, has arrived in London from Yorkshire, accompanied by his niece, Miss Petula Buckden, who is to make her curtsey at Buckingham House to Their Majesties. Sir Roderick Buckden has taken 47 Berkeley Square for the Season, where he will entertain.

They had all moved to Berkeley Square from Mrs. Warren's small house in Islington as soon as Petula had enough new gowns to wear.

The house, she learnt, belonged in fact to one of Mrs. Warren's relations, who was ill in the country and was therefore prepared to rent it to Sir Roderick.

It was impressive, well furnished, and the right background, Petula knew, for an heiress.

Everything happened so quickly that it was only when she was alone at night in the darkness of her room that she shivered and felt terrified of the future.

Sometimes she wanted to slip out of the house and find her way back to Annie and all that remained of the safety and security she had once known.

But she knew that the money she had left with her old Nurse would not last forever and that a rich husband would mean that she must support not only her uncle but also Annie and Adam.

Living so quietly in Yorkshire, she had not realised that gentlemen could be so smart, so elegant, and at the same time so overwhelming.

Not in the way the Major had been—that was different—but in making her feel tongue-tied and stupid and wondering wildly how she could reply to the fulsome compliments they paid her.

'It is because I am so ignorant,' she thought.

At the same time, the thought of having to marry any of the men whom she had met so far made her feel as if she were being dragged down into a quicksand from which there could be no escape.

One consolation was that Mrs. Warren was so kind and in a way understanding.

"I know this must seem a very strange life to you, dear," she said in her gentle way, "especially after your father was ill for so long and you saw so few people while you were nursing him. But you will get used to it."

"I suppose so," Petula said, "but the men I sit next to at dinner talk about things I have never heard of, and I cannot understand their jokes."

Privately Mrs. Warren thought that this was a good thing, but aloud she said:

"All you have to do is to look lovely, and everyone is already acclaiming you as the most beautiful débutante of the Season."

"That is what Uncle Roderick . . . hoped I would . . . be."

"Your uncle is always right," Mrs. Warren said, "so just do as he says. He is so anxious for you to be a success."

Petula wondered what Mrs. Warren would think if she knew what her uncle really desired. She felt ashamed that they must deceive this kind, understanding woman as well as everyone else.

"What does it feel like to be a great heiress?" one of the gentlemen she had met last night asked her.

"I still feel very much the same as I did before," Petula answered truthfully.

He laughed.

"You must not get your head turned by being in the position to buy anything that takes your fancy."

"I hope not," Petula said.

"It is a very beautiful head whatever it does," he said, "but I am sure you are tired of people telling you so."

"I only feel uncomfortable when I feel that they are being insincere," Petula retorted.

"Which I could never be," he answered.

He was about to say something else but then Sir Roderick joined them, and in what seemed an obvious manner to Petula he drew her aside.

"That young man is of no use to you," he said, "so do not waste your time."

Petula felt it was horrible to think that she could only talk and be pleasant to someone if she was trying to get something out of them, which in her case meant a proposal of marriage.

Then she told herself that she was well aware, as her uncle was, that the money he had obtained from the sale of the house and the estate would not last forever—certainly not at the rate they were spending it, although it was only on what her uncle considered necessities.

"Will people think it strange, if I am so rich, that I do not give them expensive presents or subscribe largely to charities?" Petula had asked.

Her uncle laughed.

"The rich are usually very close-fisted," he replied. "They think it enough for you to be in their company without having to distribute largesse! Anyway, a woman never has to put her hand into her pocket. Leave all that to me."

Petula thought that was easy, considering that she had never had a penny of her own and even had to ask her uncle for money to place on the collection plate in Church on Sunday.

Again, it was not the sort of Service she was used to, quiet and sincere, in the little grey stone Church in Buckden where she had been christened.

Everyone who was fashionable, she learnt, worshipped on Sunday morning at Saint George's Hanover Square, in pews that were inscribed with their names and for which they paid a considerable rent.

It was more of a fashion parade than a Service. The congregation greeted one another without lowering their voices.

The women inspected and criticised one another's gowns, and Petula even heard several of the gentlemen exchanging racing tips.

It was hard to pray as she always had from the depths of her heart or to talk to her mother, who she had always felt was especially near to her in Church.

When they walked down the aisle she found herself unaccountably beside Lord Crowhurst, who was asking when he could see her again.

As she might have expected, her uncle replied for her, and she suddenly had the uncomfortable thought that Lord Crowhurst was menacing her in a way that made her feel as if he were a dark cloud shutting out the sunshine.

"What are we doing today?" Mrs. Warren asked now as they sat in the Morning-Room in Berkeley Square.

It was a charming room overlooking a small paved garden at the back with a fountain playing in the spring sunshine.

71

"Crowhurst suggested that he would drive us down to Ranelagh," Sir Roderick replied.

Petula felt her heart drop.

"But I refused his offer," he went on. "Instead, His Lordship is waiting impatiently to see Petula tonight, when we go to the biggest Ball to which we have been invited so far."

"She must wear one of her prettiest gowns," Mrs. Warren exclaimed.

"Exactly!" Sir Roderick agreed. "And as I want both you ladies to look your best, I suggest you rest after I have taken you for a short drive in the park."

"That will be lovely!" Mrs. Warren exclaimed.

There was an expression in her eyes which told Petula how much she longed to be with her uncle.

"We are not tiring you too much, Elaine?" he asked.

"No, of course not!" she replied. "You know how exciting it is for me to go to all these parties, which I refused ever since I became a widow, because I had no escort."

Sir Roderick smiled at her and for a moment it seemed to Petula as if they had forgotten that she was in the room.

Then he rose to his feet and said:

"Petula has undoubtedly made little ripples amongst the *Beau Monde*, but it is not enough. Tonight I intend her to meet Temple Coombe."

"The Earl?" Mrs. Warren questioned in a puzzled tone.

"The Earl!" Sir Roderick repeated. "He has been a widower for five years and is desperate to have an heir."

"But he is far too old . . ." Mrs. Warren began.

They talked, Petula thought, as if she were not there and had no part in what was being planned for her.

Because she felt she could not bear it she slipped away from the room, and neither Sir Roderick nor Mrs. Warren seemed to be aware that she had left them.

As she walked up the finely carpeted staircase to her own bed-room she was thinking not of whom she would meet this evening but of the Major.

There had hardly been a moment since leaving Yorkshire that he had not been in her thoughts, and she knew that she compared him to all the men she met, to their disadvantage.

She had thought that perhaps he would be in London and she would see him if only from a distance.

Then she told herself firmly that he had said they would never meet again and she must accept that and not fight against what was obviously his decision.

And yet he had kissed her!

Every night she fell asleep pretending that she was in his arms and his lips were on hers.

Sometimes she dreamt of him and awoke to feel that sensation of wonder and glory which he had evoked in her and which it was impossible to forget.

"How can I ever feel like that for anyone else?" she asked herself despairingly.

Then she told herself she had to accept the fact that it had been a dream, a moment of enchantment that could never come again.

And yet, inevitably, as she dressed for the Ball they were to attend, she wondered what the Major would say if he could see her in the exquisite gown that her uncle and Mrs. Warren had chosen for her to wear.

It was white, as was traditional for a débutante, but with a difference in that it was trimmed with white camelias round the hem of the slim, almost transparent skirt.

The new fashion, which had been introduced in Paris by the Empress Josephine and had only recently come to London, had both surprised and shocked Petula.

Never had she imagined that a lady could reveal so much of her figure and yet be considered respectable.

Because she was slim and graceful, the high-waisted gowns that had something Grecian in their flowing lines made her look like a young goddess.

When artificial camelias had been affixed to her hair she might have posed for a statue of Aphrodite.

Mrs. Warren, in a gown the colour of Parma violets and wearing a small tiara, looked very aristocratic, and Petula was bound to admit that her uncle in his evening-clothes made most of his contemporaries look heavy and older in years than their age.

The expensive carriage that her uncle had hired for the Season was drawn by two well-bred horses, and the coachman and footman in their cockaded hats afforded them an air of affluence.

'If people only knew the truth,' Petula thought as she had thought a thousand times before.

Then she told herself it was stupid to keep worrying that they might be found out and exposed.

If they were, she was quite certain that her uncle would find a very plausible explanation as to why suddenly she had ceased to be an heiress.

She had learnt how cleverly he had spread the rumour of her wealth.

"When your uncle came into White's Club," one of his friends said to her, "to throw himself down in a chair and say: 'I wager a monkey that not one of you will be able to guess what has happened to me!' we all laughed.

"One or two of us hazarded a suggestion," he went on.

He saw that Petula was listening and continued:

"Then your uncle exclaimed: 'You are all wrong! You see before you the Guardian, the protector, and the administrator of the huge fortune of the most incredibly beautiful girl I have ever seen.'

"Of course we were curious," the story-teller said. "And then he told us that he had brought you to London for the Season."

"Uncle Roderick has been very kind to me," Petula said, feeling that some response was expected from her.

"There is no reason why he should not be," was the answer.

She knew from the dry note in the voice of her uncle's friend that he was thinking that Sir Roderick was enjoying living luxuriously as he had been unable to do in the past.

Now that she had been in London for over a week Petula could understand how the story her uncle had told in White's Club had spread swiftly round the other Clubs and amongst the ladies who led Society.

As soon as they moved into Berkeley Square, invitations began to arrive. Over some of them Mrs. Warren shook her head.

"They are not the sort of people Petula should know," she would say gently.

Immediately Sir Roderick would tear up the invitation and throw it into the waste-paper basket.

"Should we not refuse?" Petula asked.

"I will not even waste the writing-paper on them," her uncle retorted.

Other of the invitations made him smile with pleasure.

"I never thought I should be invited to the Lennoxes," he said to Mrs. Warren. "It is amazing how the mere smell of money greases the wheels."

"You must not be so cynical," Mrs. Warren replied. "You know as well as I do that the Marquis has four unmarried sons and the eldest will inherit everything."

Sir Roderick had handed the invitation to Petula.

"Accept with pleasure!" he ordered.

When Mrs. Warren left the room he added:

"You need not be interested in the young men for whom the party is being given. Concentrate on their friends."

His remark made Petula feel embarrassed and also contributed to her shyness.

She was not aware that because she looked so young, shy, and innocent, men found her irresistible.

They gravitated towards her not only because they thought she was so rich but because she seemed a little helpless and in need of protection.

"I may be a fool in many ways," she heard her uncle say once to Mrs. Warren, "but I am an infallible judge of horses and women. I knew the moment I saw Petula that she was a winner and I am right."

"You are indeed!" Mrs. Warren replied. "All the Dowagers tonight were saying how sweet and modest she is, and not in the least uppish or pretentious because she has such a large fortune."

She smiled at Petula as she said:

"I would like to tell you, dearest child, what a pleasure it is to chaperon someone who is admired not only by the gentlemen but also by the ladies."

Petula blushed, and once again she wondered what Mrs. Warren would think if she knew the truth and realised she was helping two tricksters to deceive those who were only being kind.

It certainly did not trouble her uncle, but it troubled her.

"Will the Prince of Wales be there tonight?" Mrs. Warren asked as the carriage drove from Berkeley Square down one of the streets which led towards Park Lane.

"Of course!" Sir Roderick replied. "So, make yourself pleasant, Elaine, to Mrs. Fitzherbert. I know you do not really approve of her. At the same time, she is a nice woman."

"There are a great many people who are shocked by her liaison with the Prince," Mrs. Warren said in a rather prim voice.

"Well, I am not one of them and I do not wish you to be either," Sir Roderick replied.

Mrs. Warren did not answer.

Petula had learnt that she could not have come to London at a better time to enjoy the entertainments and the extravagances of the London Season.

76

After nine years of war the Amiens Treaty had brought a cessation of hostilities between France and England, and not only Society but the people as a whole rejoiced at the return of peace and plenty.

Houses that had been shuttered and closed because the master or the eldest son was with his Regiment were now open.

The Prince of Wales at Carlton House set an example of lavish entertaining and extravagance which was followed by all those who wished to be in the fashion.

Outside the huge mansion where they would be entertained tonight, Petula saw the long stream of painted carriages drawn by horses with silver bridles and manned by servants in the most gorgeous gold-braided livery.

There were linkmen with flaring torches and flunkeys in powdered wigs outside the porticoed door, and a red carpet spread up the steps and into a brilliantly lit hall.

Here, waiting to proceed up the double staircase, was a crowd of guests more splendidly dressed and sumptuously bejewelled than Petula had ever seen at any previous party.

Chandeliers glowing with a thousand candles heated the rooms, and there was the heavy fragrance of flowers and the scent of exotic Parisian perfumes to make the air seem almost stifling.

The chatter of voices and the laughter of the ladies seemed to mingle with the glitter of the decorations and the sparkle of tiaras that were almost like crowns on every fashionably dressed head.

If to Petula it was a spectacle, to Sir Roderick it was a conclave of friends. He seemed to know everyone present and introduced Petula to so many different people that she felt bewildered even before they had begun to climb the staircase.

There was no doubt that the surroundings were a perfect background for the guests.

There were pictures which she felt sure were

77

priceless masterpieces, and when they reached the top of the staircase there was furniture that she longed to examine, as they moved on towards the open doors of what was obviously a huge Salon.

Now she could hear the stentorian tones of the Master of Ceremonies announcing the guests:

"Viscount and Viscountess Loftus! His Excellency the Russian Ambassador and the Princess de Lieven! The Earl and Countess of Berkeley!"

Then their turn came.

"The Honourable Mrs. Warren, Miss Petula Buckden, and Sir Roderick Buckden!"

Mrs. Warren was shaking hands with a distinguished white-haired woman wearing a diamond tiara and a huge necklace of the same stones.

"How lovely to see you again, dear Elaine. I am delighted that you have brought Miss Buckden with you. I have heard so much about her."

As she spoke she held out a gloved hand to Petula, who sank in a low curtsey.

"I hope you will enjoy your first Season," her hostess said kindly. "You must meet my daughter Emelye, who has just arrived in London."

Petula shook hands with a rather attractive girl, taller than she, who had a surprisingly hearty handgrip and whose face was unmistakably sun-tanned.

"I hear you come from Yorkshire," she said. "It is strange that we have never met, do you not think so, Adrian?"

She turned her head as she spoke to the man standing next to her in the receiving line and automatically Petula looked at him at the same time.

Suddenly she felt as if she had been turned to stone and it was impossible to breathe or move.

It was the Major who stood there, tall, overwhelming, seeming to dwarf everything and everyone by his mere presence.

Far away, so faintly that she could hardly hear what was being said, the girl who was called Emelye was saying:

"Let me introduce you to my fiancé, the Duke of Donchester—Miss Petula Buckden!"

Almost as if someone invisible forced her to bend her knees, Petula curtseyed and the man facing her bowed.

She could not put out her hand to touch his and she felt, as he did not move, that he too was finding it hard to breathe.

For a moment Petula met his eyes. Then as if it were all happening a very long way away, she realised that Mrs. Warren was waiting for her and she moved on.

She could not see the crowded room or the people who packed it. She felt as if everything were swimming in front of her, covered by a mist, so that it was impossible to distinguish anything or anyone.

"Are you all right?" Mrs. Warren asked. "You look very pale."

"I ... I think it is ... the heat," Petula managed to reply.

Mrs. Warren led the way across the room to an open window.

"It is very stifling on the stairs," she said sympathetically, "but you will be all right in a moment."

"Y-yes ... yes, of course," Petula murmured.

"Would you like your uncle to fetch you a glass of water?"

"No ... no, I am ... all right."

As if to give her time to fight what must be a slight faintness, Mrs. Warren looked down into the garden below.

"How pretty it is with the fairy-lights," she said. "One might almost be in the country."

Her words made Petula think of the wood where the Major had kissed her.

The sun had been percolating through the green leaves of the silver birch trees, and it had been part of the glory and wonder of his kiss.

He had said they would never meet again, but he was here, here in this room, and he was engaged to the girl who had given her a hearty hand-shake, the girl with the sun-tanned face.

Her uncle joined them and there was a series of further introductions.

She did not hear their names, and she did not know what they said to her or what she replied.

Later they moved from the Reception-Rooms down another staircase to the Ball-Room—a large room built out at the back of the house and opening onto the garden.

Petula danced but all the time she was watching the door, waiting to see one person and one person only.

Then, she was not certain how it happened, she found herself in the garden with Lord Crowhurst.

"At last I have you to myself," he was saying in his thick voice.

"I . . . I think Uncle Roderick is looking for me," Petula said automatically.

"Forget your uncle," Lord Crowhurst replied. "I want to talk to you without him giving me the answers."

Petula realised that they were standing under the branches of a tree which was lit by hanging Chinese lanterns.

They were not far from the Ball-Room and there were couples either talking or walking all round them, so she was not afraid.

She only felt it was an unutterable bore to have to listen to this man when she wanted to think, wanted to understand why Major Adrian Chester was in reality the Duke of Donchester.

'No wonder he looked so aloof and disdainful when I first saw him in the garden,' she thought, 'but afterwards . . .'

She shut her eyes for the moment and heard Lord Crowhurst say with a note of concern in his voice:

"I did not mean to upset you, I only wanted you to know how much you mean to me already."

Petula put out her hand as if to find something to hold on to and he guided her to a seat directly beneath the tree.

"It is the heat," he said. "People always ask too many guests and the whole thing becomes an intolerable crush as it is at Carlton House. I will fetch you a glass of champagne."

He moved away as he spoke and Petula shut her eyes, grateful that he had gone, because she wanted to think.

"Petula!"

There was no mistaking the voice that spoke to her and her eyes opened to find him towering over her, his dark head silhouetted against a Chinese lantern.

Automatically she rose to her feet and felt him take her hand in his.

"I must speak to you!"

She looked over her shoulder.

"Lord Crowhurst has ... gone to ... fetch me some ... champagne."

Without speaking, the Duke drew her round the back of the tree and across the lawn towards some shrubs that were in shadows.

Only when they were out of the range of the lanterns and there were only a few fairy-lights near them did he stop.

He had taken her hand but now he released it and she raised her eyes to his face, which she could see quite clearly by the light of the moon, which was just climbing up the sky.

"Why are you here?" the Duke asked.

His voice sounded accusing and Petula said quickly:

"Please ... I beg of you ... do not say that we have ... met or where you ... found me. Uncle ... Roderick will be very ... angry if you do so."

"I understand now that your uncle is Sir Roderick Buckden," he said, "but I did not connect him with you when I came to the Manor. I do not know him well, but he is a member of my Club."

It was almost as if he spoke to himself to clarify in his own mind what he knew, and Petula murmured:

"You s-said we would . . . never m-meet again."

"But we have met, Petula, and I am trying to ascertain what has happened."

"You must not . . . ask questions," she said quickly. "I did not . . . tell Uncle Roderick you had stayed at the Manor . . . therefore no-one must ever . . . know about me . . . please. . . ."

"But you will tell me."

She shook her head.

"Why not?" he asked.

Petula drew in a deep breath.

"Because the . . . man who came was a . . . Major who had been in the . . . Army."

"That was true enough," the Duke said. "I was a Major in the Army, and when I am travelling it is easier to do so incognito."

"It . . . must be, but . . ."

He saw in her eyes what she wanted to say and he asked almost abruptly:

"How could I know that the wheel of my Phaeton would be damaged and I would meet you? I have tried to forget you, Petula, but it has been impossible!"

She did not reply and after a moment he said in a different tone:

"Have you thought about me?"

As if he compelled her to answer, Petula said in a voice he could hardly hear:

"Y-yes . . ."

"Often?"

"All . . . all the . . . time."

She saw a sudden light in his eyes.

"How then can you ask me to forget?"

"It was . . . a dream, as you said . . . and we had to go . . . back to . . . reality."

"But this is real and you are here."

"I know . . . but . . ."

"But! But! But!" he said. "I know what you are thinking, and I am thinking the same, but I could

82

not help it, Petula. I lay awake that night wanting you so unbearably that all the will-power and self-control in the world could not prevent me from coming to find you the next morning."

He paused and looked down at her, at her eyes in the moonlight seeming to glow with a light which came from within and which made her radiate a strange enchantment which swept what he was about to say from his lips.

"How could I anticipate for one moment that this would happen to me?" he asked hoarsely.

"Wh-what do you ... mean?"

"I mean that I fell in love," he replied. "I fell in love with you, and God knows, although I have tried, I cannot get you out of my mind or out of my heart."

He thought it was impossible for any woman to look as beautiful as Petula did when transformed by his words.

"Y-you ... love me?"

She hardly breathed the words, and yet he heard them.

"I love you," he replied. "I knew it before I kissed you, but when I felt your lips meet mine I knew that we belonged to each other. Yet there was nothing, believe me, Petula, there was nothing I could do about it."

"I ... loved you too," she whispered. "I was ... afraid to admit it, but that is what I have been feeling ... love. And it is .... different from what I ... expected."

"My precious! My darling!" he said. "Oh, God, how much I love you!"

He did not move, but she felt that he drew nearer to her and almost instinctively she put up her hands as if to ward him off.

"I will not touch you," he said, "though Heaven knows it is a hell not to do so, but I have to see you. Where are you? Where can we meet?"

"Uncle Roderick ..." Petula began.

"I have to see you," the Duke interrupted. "I have to talk to you. There is so much to explain, and yet I feel you understand."

He looked across the garden almost as if he felt that people were encroaching upon them.

"I must go back," he said, "and so must you, but tell me where we can meet—anytime, anywhere."

"I . . . I could slip out very early tomorrow morning, about five o'clock," Petula said, "but I do not know where . . . to suggest I should . . . go."

She spoke helplessly and the Duke moved a step forward as if he would take her in his arms to protect her. Then he said:

"I will be waiting for you in a closed carriage at the corner of Charles Street. Just walk round the corner of Berkeley Square and get into it!"

His voice sharpened as he went on:

"If they discover that you have left the house we will have to think up some explanation, but come to me, for God's sake, Petula! Come to me or I think I shall go mad!"

"I will . . . come!" she promised.

Then it seemed as if he faded away into the shadows and left her so quickly that for a moment she thought he was not real but she had dreamt his presence beside her.

Then as she moved back towards the tree with the Chinese lanterns she saw Lord Crowhurst, with a glass in his hand, looking for her. . . .

Chapter Five

Soon after dawn Petula got out of bed and dressed.

She had not been able to sleep despite the fact that they had come home early.

Her uncle had been angry with her. Just as she joined Lord Crowhurst he had come from the house with a black look on his face which told her he was incensed.

"Where have you been, Petula?" he asked sharply. "There was someone I wished you to meet and I could not find you."

"It was so hot, Uncle Roderick . . ." Petula began, only to be interrupted by Lord Crowhurst, who said:

"I am afraid your niece felt faint, Buckden, and it is not surprising, seeing that as usual there are far too many people crushed into far too small a space."

Her uncle did not answer; he merely took her by the arm and led her back towards the house.

As they neared the entrance he said in a low voice:

"Surely you have enough sense to know you should not go into the garden alone with a man?"

Petula did not reply. It had been difficult enough ever since arriving at the Ball and meeting the Duke to think about or concentrate on anything but him. Now that she had talked to him, it was doubly difficult.

Her uncle had introduced her to several people who were standing with Mrs. Warren, and it was only later that she realised she had not heard their names nor could she even remember what they looked like.

She thought she had talked to several other people but she was not sure. All she could think of was that the Duke loved her as she loved him.

"He loves me," she whispered beneath her breath.

She felt herself thrill even though she knew he belonged to the girl with the sun-tanned face.

At last after what seemed an interminable length of time she was back in her own bed and the room was in darkness.

Only then did she realise, now that she had found again the man who by his kiss awoke such an ecstasy and glory within her, that it would be even more agonising to lose him for the second time.

He loved her!

Over and over again she found herself remembering the deep note in his voice when he said:

"I fell in love with you, and God knows, although I have tried, I cannot get you out of my mind or out of my heart."

He loved her! Could anything, Petula asked herself, be more incredible and at the same time more utterly and completely wonderful?

She lay awake, her heart throbbing tumultuously in her breasts, and felt as if once again his lips were on hers in the quietness and beauty of the little wood where he had opened the gates of Heaven to her.

As she dressed she knew that nothing and nobody would stop her from going to him as he had asked her to do. At the same time, she was sure she could leave the house unobserved.

In most houses, especially those as grand as the one which her uncle had rented, there was always a footman and a night-watchman on duty.

But because Sir Roderick was economising in every possible way that would not be noticed behind the impressive facade he put on, the actual household consisted of very few permanent staff.

When there was a dinner-party extra servants were hired for the occasion and so was the Chef.

At other times there was just a plain cook who made no pretensions of doing anything elaborate, while an elderly man who had been trained as a Butler and his wife kept the rooms comparatively clean.

None of them, Petula knew, would be about at this hour of the morning, although Annie had often told her that in grand houses the under-housemaids and the kitchen staff were always up by five o'clock.

Wearing one of the plainest gowns she possessed, but which was still to her both lovely and elaborate, and a straw bonnet trimmed simply with blue ribbons, Petula slipped noiselessly down the staircase.

It was not difficult to slide back the bolts on the front door, and she thought that if Bruton, the Butler, found them undone he would merely suppose he had been absent-minded the night before.

Berkeley Square was deserted. Later it would be filled with lavender-sellers, organ-grinders, and crossing-sweepers, besides, like every other street in London, a large number of beggars.

Many of them were maimed and crippled men who had been discharged from the Army or the Navy without being properly recompensed by the country for which they had fought.

It was only a short distance to Charles Street and Petula hurried along, thinking it unlikely that anyone would see her but knowing that if one of their neighbours did so they would think it extraordinary that she was unchaperoned.

Then as she rounded the corner she saw a carriage waiting.

It was a small brougham, quiet and unostentatious, without painted panels and not even identifiable by a crest.

There were two men on the box and one of them jumped down as soon as she appeared.

As he opened the door of the carriage she saw that it was Jason, and he touched his hat as Petula, too shy to acknowledge him, stepped into the carriage.

A hand came out to assist her, the door shut behind her, and almost immediately the horses moved off.

She half-turned to raise her eyes to the man beside her and realised that he was looking at her in the same searching manner.

"You came!" he said. "I was afraid something might stop you."

"I . . . wanted to see . . . you."

She thought her voice sounded strangely unlike her own, but her whole body was pulsatingly aware of the Duke, of his closeness and that they were alone.

Because she was shy of her own emotions she said in an effort to appear natural:

"You are . . . still in evening . . . dress."

He smiled.

"I had no time to change. My last guest only left about half an hour ago."

He saw the question in her eyes and added:

"Did you not know that it was to my house you came?"

"N-no . . . I did not know . . . I did not even know who had . . . invited us," Petula replied.

"You have to explain—you have to tell me what has happened," the Duke said.

As she did not answer he went on:

"When I saw you tonight I thought I must be dreaming; in fact I have dreamt of you so often that I find your face everywhere I look."

Petula quivered and he took her hand in both of his and held it closely.

"You are more beautiful than I remember," he said, "and yet it would be impossible for anyone to be more lovely than you were when I kissed you in the wood."

She felt her fingers tremble in his.

"Petula—what has happened to us?" he asked. "And what are we to do about it?"

"What ... can we ... do?"

She found it hard even to breathe the words.

"Do you suppose I have not been thinking of every possibility since I left you standing on the steps, looking so forlorn and lost and at the same time so incredibly, heart-breakingly beautiful?"

Petula drew in her breath, then she said hesitatingly:

"Y-you are ... to be ... married!"

"I was on my way to Kirkby Castle," the Duke replied, "for my engagement to be announced first to the Earl's relatives. Then we were all to return to London for the Ball you attended last night."

He paused, and she heard the pain, sharp as a knife, in his voice as he said:

"The announcement appears in the Court Circular this morning."

The pressure of his fingers on hers was painful as he went on:

"It is something which has been planned for years. In fact ever since I was twenty-one, or perhaps before that. My father and the Earl were close friends."

"Do you ... love her?"

The Duke knew it was the one question Petula needed to ask.

"I am fond of Emelye," he answered, "and I have known her since a child. We have many tastes in common. She loves horses and so do I, and she is a magnificent rider."

He saw the expression in Petula's eyes and added:

"But I have never been in love, my darling, and this is the truth, until I met you."

"How can we ... love each ... other?" Petula asked.

"Your question should be—how can we help it?" the Duke replied. "It happened so swiftly that I thought I must be imagining the whole thing."

He gave a deep sigh.

"Then when I touched you, when I kissed you, I knew that all the stories about love at first sight—of being overwhelmed, bewitched and infatuated to the point of madness—were true."

"I ... I felt the same," Petula whispered, "but it is ... wrong, because you ... belong to ... someone else."

"It is not wrong, my precious," the Duke said. "It is just that there seems to be nothing honourable I can do about it."

Petula turned her face to look at him and he said with a sudden violence she had never heard from him before:

"God Almighty, what am I to do? Give me the answer."

Because he frightened her a little she would have taken her hand from his but he held on to it.

"I am sorry. Forgive me!" he said. "I cannot think of you and remain sane."

As he spoke he raised her hand in both of his and kissed it and she felt that indescribable sensation that he had aroused in her before rise in her breasts and into her throat.

"I love you!" he said. "And I know when I look into your eyes, as I knew before I left your house, that you love me a little."

"Yes ... I love ... you!" Petula murmured. "But you are ... betrothed."

She felt as she spoke as if she struck at him, but he kissed the back of her hand once again before, still holding it in both of his, he put it down on his knee.

"Now tell me about yourself," he said. "Last night when you were dancing Emelye said to me: 'That is the Yorkshire heiress everyone is talking about. I cannot think why I have not met her. I thought as Papa is Lord Lieutenant I knew everyone in Yorkshire!'"

Petula did not answer and the Duke said:

"Where did all this money come from? How could it have happened so quickly?"

"I . . . I cannot . . . tell you."

"Why not?"

"Because it is not only . . . my secret."

"Why should there be a secret?" the Duke asked. "When I saw your house I realised that you were very poor, at least I thought so."

Petula was silent and after a moment he said:

"There cannot be any mysteries or secrets between us. Tell me, Petula, what happened."

"It is . . . better for you not to . . . know," she answered, "and as you are well aware . . . we must not . . . see each other again."

"How can I bear it? How can I live knowing you are in London, looking for you at every party I attend, at every place I go?"

"Then . . . perhaps I should go . . . away."

Even as she spoke she wondered wildly how she could achieve it. What would her uncle say after he had spent so much money on her clothes, the house, and the whole masquerade?

"As I told you last night, I have met your uncle," the Duke said. "I know he is a gambler who has not appeared to have much money until now. Where has it come from? And why are you spoken of as an heiress?"

"Please," Petula pleaded, "please . . . do not probe and ask questions. I do not want to tell you . . . why I am here . . . I do not . . . want you to know."

"What has happened to the Manor?" the Duke asked.

Because the question took her by surprise Petula told him the truth.

"Uncle Roderick sold it."

She saw a speculative look come into the Duke's eyes and added quickly:

"Perhaps I should . . . not have said . . . that. Forget . . . it!"

"I think I am beginning to understand," he said slowly. "Your uncle sold the house and the estate, and then, seeing how beautiful you are, he brought you to London."

His hands tightened on hers until she gave a little cry.

"What for?" he asked. "Tell me what for!"

The colour rose in Petula's cheeks but she could not speak.

"I know the answer," he said bitterly. "For a rich husband! It is obvious, is it not?"

Once again his voice was violent.

"How could you do such a thing? How could you lower yourself to seek a husband by such means?"

"I ... I could not help it," Petula answered. "If I had not ... done as Uncle Roderick said, he would have ... left me to ... starve."

The tears gathered in her eyes and the Duke put his arm round her and pulled her against him.

"My sweet! My darling! I have made you cry," he said. "How can I be such a brute? I understand, of course I understand, but how can I see you married to someone else?"

His arm holding her close against him gave her an inexpressible feeling of security, and without really meaning to do so she put her head against his shoulder.

With his free hand he undid the ribbons of her bonnet and pulling it from her head threw it onto the floor of the carriage. Then he said, his voice low and tender:

"Let me look at you! I shall never forgive myself for having made you cry."

He wiped away the tears which had fallen onto her cheeks, then he said:

"Tell me everything, for I have to know."

Hesitantly, at the same time feeling that it was impossible to do anything but what he wished, Petula told him how her uncle had arrived at Buckden.

She related how he had sold the estate, and although she had suggested staying there with Annie, he had insisted that she should come to London so that he could find her a rich husband.

She knew by the way the Duke's arm tightened about her and the expression on his face as he listened that he was shocked and even appalled by her uncle's plan.

At the same time, there was a relief in knowing that at any rate she need not pretend to him.

When she finished speaking he was silent, and after a moment she said pathetically:

"Because of what I have ... told you ... you will not stop .... loving me?"

"Do you really think that would be possible?" he asked. "If you committed murder, if you were accused of every crime in the calendar, I should still love you because I cannot help myself."

He looked into her eyes and said:

"When I drove away, telling myself I must forget you, I left my heart behind."

"And you took ... mine with ... you," Petula whispered.

Slowly, as if it was inevitable, the Duke's lips found hers.

For a moment he was very gentle. Then as he had done before in the garden he pulled her closer still and his kiss became demanding, insistent, and utterly and completely possessive.

She knew that he held her captive. She was his and where their feelings were concerned there was no escape for either of them.

They belonged; they were one person.

When the Duke raised his head he thought that while Petula had been lovely before, at this moment she seemed to shine with an inner radiance that had something celestial about it.

"I love you!" he said hoarsely. "There are no other words to express what I feel."

Barbara Cartland

"And I ... love ... you!" Petula answered, and hid
her face against his shoulder.

She felt him touch her hair gently and realised
the carriage had come to a standstill.

She turned her head and saw through the window that they had stopped by some trees at the side
of the Serpentine.

There was no-one about and it was very quiet.

The light of the early sun was percolating through
the branches and shining on the silvery water, and
made her think of the wood and how it was there
that she had first been aware of her love.

As if the Duke followed her thoughts he said:

"I have thought about you every day and every
night, and while I kept telling myself it was wrong
to do so I knew that eventually it would be impossible for me not to return to you."

"It would be wrong ... because you are to be ...
married," Petula said.

"I know," the Duke replied, "but what can I do?
My darling, my dream come true, tell me, what can I
do?"

"There is ... nothing," Petula answered. "As you
said yourself ... nothing honourable."

"I torture myself that if I had been brave enough
to take you away with me it might have been possible," the Duke said.

"They were waiting for you at Kirkby Castle?"

"Yes, and the Earl's relatives of course had already been told of the engagement before my arrival."

"Then there is nothing you could have done."

"How could I have been such a fool," he asked,
"as to agree to a marriage without love? My only excuse is that I did not know that love such as I have
for you existed except in the imagination of some
poet."

He put his hand under Petula's chin and turned
her face up to his.

"How can you be so absurdly lovely?" he said.
"How can everything you say and do tug at the heart

94

I did not know I possessed? How can your lips give me an awareness of the Heaven in which I had ceased to believe?"

"That is . . . what I feel about you," Petula said, "but I never . . . never dreamt that you would . . . feel the same."

"And now that you know I do?"

"I am proud . . . so very proud that you should . . . love me."

"But how can we exist without each other?"

He stared at the still water shining in the early sun as if he thought it would give him a solution. Then because she knew how desperate he felt Petula said quietly:

"You must do what is . . . right. After all, you are very . . . important and I am . . . nobody. It would damage your . . . reputation if we were talked . . . about."

"If we could be talked about it would make me the happiest man in the world," the Duke said.

He gave a deep sigh, then he added:

"If you were really nobody, then it might be easier; but I knew at Buckden that the only position I could offer you in my life would be that of my wife."

Petula was silent for a moment, then she said:

"I . . . I think I understand. You mean . . . if I had really been nobody you might have asked me to be your . . . mistress."

The Duke pulled her roughly against him.

"I would not spoil anything that is so perfect by such a suggestion," he said. "As I have already said, Petula, if it had been possible I would have come back and asked if you would honour me by being my wife."

As he spoke his lips found hers again and he kissed her until the world seemed to swing round her and she was unconscious of everything except him and the wonder he evoked in her.

Finally, when he released her, she could only

look up at him with her breath coming brokenly through her parted lips, her eyes seeming to hold all the sunshine in their depths.

"I love . . . you! Oh, I . . . love you!" she cried, and the Duke said:

"If you look at me like that, I shall carry you away with me here and now, and damn the consequences!"

There was a passion in his words which did not make Petula afraid but feel as if she vibrated to music.

Then she said:

"If you will not think of . . . yourself, then I must think for . . . you. We must . . . say good-bye . . . and we must try . . . to forget."

"That is impossible!" the Duke said sharply. "Do you think I can forget that you are looking for a husband, that some other man will touch you, kiss you, and make you his?"

He felt the quiver of revulsion that ran through Petula and said:

"If it kills me to think of it, what will it do to you, my darling? For I know you love me, and I know you belong to me spiritually."

"Perhaps I could . . . run away and hide . . . somewhere," Petula suggested.

"For the rest of your life?" the Duke asked. "My precious, it would be impossible, wherever you hid, for some man not to see you. Even if he arrived unexpectedly after an accident to his Phaeton!"

He tried to smile, but instead there was an agony in his eyes that made Petula press herself a little closer to him as she said:

"We must not . . . regret. At least we have . . . known how wonderful . . . love can be. No-one can take that . . . away from . . . us."

"It may seem of some consolation to you," the Duke replied. "But I think love has inflicted on me a torture more intense, more cruel, than I could ever express in words."

"No . . . please . . ." Petula protested, "you must

not ... think like that. If I had never ... met you, if you had never ... kissed me, I should not have ... known that love is the most ... perfect ... the most ... beautiful thing in the world and part ... of God Himself!"

The Duke made a little sound that was almost like a broken cry.

Then he held her close against him, his lips on her hair, his eyes looking unseeingly at the shining water.

For a moment Petula pretended that they were together and that no-one could separate them. Then she forced herself to say in a voice hardly above a whisper:

"I think ... I must go ... back."

"I would not want you to get into trouble," the Duke said, "but, darling, I must see you again."

Petula shook her head.

"I may ... harm you."

"You are thinking of me!" he said. "My precious, was there ever anyone like you?"

"I love you!" Petula replied. "But because you are a Duke, because you are of such importance, you must not do anything which would shock people or make them sneer at you. I could not ... bear it! I could not bear to be a ... part of that!"

"If you are thinking of me, then I am thinking of you," he said, "and, my darling, of the sort of husband your uncle will choose for you."

Petula thought of Lord Crowhurst and turned her face so that the Duke could not see the expression in her eyes.

"I have no right to ask questions," he said, "except that you have given me the right because you love me."

He paused before asking:

"Is there nothing I can do? Suppose I gave you some money? Would that make things any better?"

Petula shook her head.

"How could I explain where the money has

come from? And we must not, as you know, be . . .
involved with . . . each other."

"But we are involved!" the Duke said fiercely.

"Only in our hearts," Petula answered quietly.
"Our minds know that already you belong to . . . someone else. Papa always said that once a man gave his
word as a gentleman it was impossible for him to
break it."

"Your father was right," the Duke said. "At the
same time, this is different."

He smiled cynically as he went on:

"What man does not say that when he is in love?
But it is different! It is different, my precious darling, because we were made for each other, because
already you belong to me and I to you."

Petula did not answer and as if he knew it was
hopeless the Duke said:

"I will take you back."

He tapped on the front of the carriage and immediately the horses began to move.

Petula looked for a moment at the trees and the
water of the Serpentine and thought that this was
another enchanted place that she would always remember because there the Duke had kissed her.

Then the horses were carrying them back through
the park, across Park Lane, and into Charles Street.

They sat in silence, the Duke holding her close
against his chest. She knew that his chin was squared
and his lips set in a tight line as they had been when
he had driven away from the Manor and left her behind.

Only as the carriage came to a standstill in
Charles Street did he say:

"I shall be thinking—thinking of some way out of
this muddle, but God alone knows what it will be."

"I shall be . . . thinking of . . . you," Petula said
softly.

"You will take care of yourself?" he asked anxiously.

She found it impossible to speak because the tears were misting her eyes.

She picked up her bonnet and put it on her head, then the Duke tied the ribbons under her chin.

His eyes looked at her hungrily, and she thought the lines on his face were sharply drawn. Then he raised her hand and laid it against his cheek, not kissing it, only holding it there.

Jason opened the door and, without speaking, without even looking back, Petula stepped out.

She had already planned not to enter the house by the front door but from the Mews.

She knew that the coachman her uncle had hired would not be particularly interested in anything she did.

As she walked over the cobble-stones with the stables on either side, she could hear the horses moving in their stalls and the grooms whistling as they rubbed them down.

She found the door which led into the Mews of number 47. There was a passage running alongside the stalls and a door which opened into another passage which led directly to the kitchen-quarters of the house.

As she had anticipated, there was no-one about and she slipped up the back stairs and found her way to her own bed-room.

There she undressed and got back into bed.

Only when she could hide her face in the pillow did she begin to cry helpless, agonising tears which seemed to come from her very soul.

* * *

"Sir Roderick would like to see you, Miss, as soon as you are dressed," Tomkins, who was Petula's lady's-maid, told her as she took away her breakfast-tray.

She was an experienced woman and therefore more expensive than any of the other servants in the household. But she was, Petula had found, a genius at arranging her hair and looking after her gowns.

"I had better get up," Petula said quickly.

"There are no engagements until after luncheon, Miss," Tomkins said, "so one of your more simple gowns will do."

Petula was not listening but merely wondering why her uncle should wish to see her. Perhaps it concerned her behaviour of the night before.

It was always difficult for him to talk to her in front of Mrs. Warren in case he said something which would reveal the part they both were playing.

Usually he drew her aside with the pretence that he had some papers for her to sign, and it was unusual for him to send messages so early in the morning.

"Perhaps he is really ... angry!" Petula told herself, and felt her heart sink.

She felt weak with the emotions she had experienced and the violence of her tears.

She washed her face very carefully, first in warm water, then in cold, and hoped her uncle would not realise she had been crying.

Tomkins arranged her hair and she went downstairs to find Sir Roderick, as she had expected, in the Library.

He was looking very smart, for he too had bought new clothes; but one glance at his expression told Petula that he was not in fact angry as she had feared but in a good humour.

"Good-morning, Petula!" he said. "I hope you enjoyed yourself last night?"

"Yes, indeed, Uncle Roderick. It was a very ... magnificent party."

"I suppose it was sheer ignorance that made you go into the garden alone with Crowhurst. You know as well as I do that you are not supposed to be alone with a man."

"I ... I am sorry ... Uncle Roderick ... it was so hot ... and I felt a little ... faint."

"I understand," Sir Roderick said, "but do not let it happen again."

"No, Uncle Roderick."

"What I want to tell you is that while you should keep Crowhurst on a string, so to speak, we have a better fish to fry."

Sir Roderick laughed.

"It sounds rather vulgar, but it expresses quite eloquently what I am trying to say."

"I do not . . . understand."

"Well, Temple Coombe, as I anticipated, is extremely interested in you."

Petula looked at him blankly.

After all the people she had met last night she was trying to recall which was the Earl of Temple Coombe.

Because she had been thinking only of the Duke, every face was just a blur and it was impossible even to remember anything anyone had said to her.

"Come along, Petula, do not be so stupid," Sir Roderick admonished. "The Earl of Temple Coombe may be slightly old, I am not denying that, but he is an extremely important man in a number of ways, and if you could bring him up to scratch—which I believe you will—then we are home and dry!"

"I am . . . afraid I do not remember the . . . gentleman."

Sir Roderick made a sound of exasperation.

"I introduced him to you after you came back from the garden. He was standing with a number of other people including Mrs. Warren. If you had been attending, which you should have been, you would have felt me press your arm. Really, Petula, at times I think you are half-witted!"

"I am . . . sorry . . . Uncle Roderick."

"I suppose I must excuse you as you were not feeling well, but frankly, this is no time for illness."

"N-no . . . I am very . . . sorry."

"I will forgive you, because we are dining with the Earl tonight."

Sir Roderick was obviously elated.

"His servant brought the invitation early this morning, which shows he is keen."

"I am glad you are pleased, Uncle Roderick."

"Pleased? I am elated! This is exactly what I had planned. Everything is going perfectly! As I have said before, I sensed what I must do where you are concerned. And I was right—yes, by God!—I was right!"

Sir Roderick walked to the desk and opening one of the drawers took out a small note-book.

"You see how carefully I have planned a campaign like this, Petula," he said. "I put down in this book the names of half a dozen men whom I intended you should meet in London."

He looked at the book with a smile on his lips as he went on:

"Only one of them has proved to be a nonstarter. There is Crowhurst already at your feet, Temple Coombe, who you will see tonight, and that leaves three others, all members of White's, who have already said that they would like to have the opportunity of meeting you."

He threw the book down on the desk and said:

"You are lucky to have a very clever uncle."

"Yes ... of course ... Uncle Roderick," Petula agreed, "and I am very ... grateful."

She tried to get the proper, enthusiastic, responsive note into her voice, but it was hard.

"You are looking tired," Sir Roderick said sharply. "There are lines under your eyes that I have not noticed before. You had better rest this afternoon."

"Have you forgotten, Uncle Roderick, that Mrs. Warren is taking me to the Drawing-Room at St. James's Palace?"

"Good Heavens—so I had!" Sir Roderick exclaimed. "Well, you certainly cannot miss that, and that reminds me, I am due at a Levée tomorrow morning. They say the King has actually recovered enough to take them himself."

He walked back to stand in front of the mantelpiece as he went on:

"Remember that St. James's is exceedingly formal. The King and Queen may live quietly at Windsor, but everything is very much *de rigueur* in London."

He paused and then said:

"Court dress is compulsory and both the King and the Queen are stuffily Royal on such occasions."

He smiled and added:

"Needless to say, the whole performance is excessively boring!"

"I am sure I shall find it interesting, Uncle Roderick."

"Doubtless you will!" Sir Roderick agreed. "But as far as I am concerned, I enjoy myself a great deal more with the Prince of Wales, however much His Majesty condemns his son's behaviour."

Petula was wondering in which camp the Duke found himself.

She had learnt as soon as she came to London that while everything social which was amusing and entertaining centred round the Prince of Wales at Carlton House, the more important aristocrats allied themselves with the King and Queen.

Even so, they admitted, as her uncle did, that the parties at Buckingham Palace, like those at St. James's Palace, were extremely dull.

'Perhaps the Duke manages not to ally himself with either group,' Petula thought.

She felt herself aching at the thought of how important he was and how hopeless it was to love someone so unfortunately above her.

Only when she escaped from her uncle and was alone could she forget everything but the fact that the Duke loved her as she loved him.

It was a joy and an agony in one.

It was a rapture—at the same time, it was a deep dark despondency to know that she could never be a part of his life or he of hers.

Perhaps, she thought, they would both be happier if she disappeared from the Social world and became his mistress.

Then she knew that such a thought was wicked and would have horrified her mother! Yet, as the

Duke had said, could such a love as they had for each other ever be wrong?

Love—real love—came, Petula was sure, from God, and it was God, not chance, that had brought them together.

It was God who had made what they felt for each other so perfect, so divine, that she knew that it was part of everything she had ever believed was sacred.

"I love him!" she told herself. "And my love is great enough to want his happiness and to know that I must not harm him in any way! Even if it means that I must never see him again."

The pain of such a thought was almost intolerable, and yet she knew she must be strong enough for both of them.

Strong enough to know they had said good-bye and there was nothing more they could say to each other.

* * *

In the afternoon, with powdered hair and wearing Court dresses with hoops, panels, and draperies, which were very different from the slim gauzes and muslins that were the fashion, Mrs. Warren and Petula drove towards St. James's Palace.

It had seemed to Petula a terrible waste of money that they should have to spend so much on gowns that they would never wear again after this one occasion when she was to make her curtsey to the Queen.

But it was all part of Sir Roderick's plan that she should be formally accepted as a débutante.

Petula learnt that a large number of invitations she had received were due to the fact that after today she would be accepted in Court Circles.

"It is quite some years since I have been to St. James's Palace," Mrs. Warren said reminiscently.

"What was the last occasion?" Petula asked.

"I was presented on my marriage."

"Were you very happy with your husband?"

Mrs. Warren hesitated for a moment before she said:

"My marriage was arranged by my father, and my husband was very much older than I was."

There was a note in her voice which told Petula now why she had protested yesterday when Sir Roderick had been talking about her meeting with Lord Temple Coombe.

"Is it much more . . . difficult to be married to an . . . older man than to a younger one?" Petula asked.

Again Mrs. Warren paused before she replied:

"Older men, especially if they have not been married before, are very set in their ways. At the same time, I expect you know the ancient adage that 'it is better to be an old man's darling than a young man's slave.' "

Petula wanted to say that she longed to be a slave to the man she loved, but she said nothing and after a moment Mrs. Warren went on:

"I know, dearest child, that your uncle is very anxious for you to marry and settle down. I have tried to persuade him that there is no need for hurry, but you know how impetuous he is."

"Yes, indeed," Petula answered.

"As you are so well endowed you should be able to take your time and find someone you love."

Petula did not speak and after a moment Mrs. Warren continued:

"If there is anyone that you love, even if he does not meet with your uncle's approval, I will try to help you, for I wish you to be happy."

Petula felt that instinctively because she was another woman Mrs. Warren sensed that she was in love.

She had a sudden impulse to tell her the truth and beg her help. Then she knew it would do no good and would only infuriate her uncle.

Mrs. Warren was almost as poor as they were and was therefore not in a position to help. Besides, how could anyone alter the impossible situation where she loved a man who was to be married to someone else?

'It is hopeless . . . hopeless!' Petula thought.

She knew that if she could not marry the Duke, then it did not really matter whom she married, for any other man would seem intolerable to her in the circumstances.

They arrived at St. James's Palace and were led by a resplendent official up the wide oak staircase to the Reception-Rooms.

Here, dressed in a similar fashion to themselves, with panniers and heavy trains hanging from their shoulders, were all the other ladies waiting either to be presented or to present their daughters.

The majority of them seemed to know Mrs. Warren, and Petula found herself curtseying and repeating over and over again how much she was enjoying her first Season in London.

Then as Mrs. Warren moved away from one old acquaintance towards another, a voice said:

"I rather expected to find you here, Elaine. I do hope you are not too tired after last night."

It was the Countess of Kirkby who was speaking and beside her Petula saw her daughter, Lady Emelye Kirk.

Then as the two older women talked together Lady Emelye said:

"Did you enjoy my party last night? Personally I thought it a terrible crush and would much rather have been in Yorkshire."

"I have not been to many Balls," Petula replied shyly, "but everyone said it was the most important and far the best that has been given so far."

"I prefer riding to dancing," Lady Emelye said. "Do you ride?"

"Yes, when I am in the country. I have not yet ridden in London."

"I should not bother," Lady Emelye said scathingly, "it is very tame, trit-trotting in the park. Papa has a miniature race-course at Kirkby and I train my horses over the jumps."

"That must be very exciting," Petula said.

"If you should want to buy some really decent hunters you had better come and see what we can show you. We have been breeding for some years and have produced some very fine horse-flesh."

She did not seem to realise that Petula had found little to say and after a moment went on:

"Well, thank goodness I can go back to York-shire the day after tomorrow. I find all this sort of thing a terrible bore, as I expect you do."

Petula was saved from answering because at that moment two Officers of State, in Court uniform and holding their Staves of Office, walked into the room backwards.

The Queen was arriving!

There was a hush that was almost one of awe, but Petula could only think that if Lady Emelye was leaving London then doubtless the Duke would go with her.

All her previous resolutions were cast away and she knew that somehow, by some means, she must see him alone—just once more.

Chapter Six

"I have not had a chance to talk to you until now," Sir Roderick said. "While Crowhurst has intimated quite clearly that he desires to marry you, Temple Coombe is still hanging fire."

He had called Petula into the Library after she and Mrs. Warren had returned from shopping.

Petula stood just inside the door, looking, although she was unconscious of it, extremely lovely in a new gown of pale green which made her look like spring itself.

She did not speak and after a moment Sir Roderick said reflectively:

"Perhaps you should give him a little more encouragement, although your recent quiet, rather detached attitude has been, I admit, extremely effective."

He walked across the room while speaking, as if it encouraged him to think, and he went on:

"So many people have congratulated me on your modest demeanour and, though at first I thought it a mistake for you to seem so distraught, it has, I must confess, been very successful."

Petula knew that he was referring to the fact that she had hardly seemed aware of what was happening round her. He was of course unaware that she could think only of one person and that was the Duke, who was to marry Lady Emelye Kirk.

It seemed to her as if no-one could talk of anything else. Even Mrs. Warren discussed the engagement incessantly and Petula found it hard to behave as if she was not personally interested.

"The Countess has always been a friend of mine," she told Petula, "and I am so delighted that their only child should make such an advantageous match."

"I hear she has known the Duke for a long time," Petula said, since Mrs. Warren obviously expected her to say something.

"Yes, indeed, ever since they were children. But I think my friend was slightly afraid that he might cry off. There have been, as you can imagine, a great many women in love with him."

Mrs. Warren laughed.

"But as they were usually sophisticated Society beauties who already had husbands, the Duke has been preserved for Emelye."

"She . . . is very . . . lucky," Petula said, and hoped her voice did not sound envious.

"She is indeed! The Duke of Donchester is not only extremely wealthy and has the most magnificent houses, like the one you saw the other evening, but he is also a very brave man."

"Brave?" Petula questioned.

"Yes, indeed," Mrs. Warren replied. "The Colonel of his Regiment was saying the other night what an excellent officer he was, and besides that the Duke is a Corinthian, and his success on the turf of course appeals to Emelye, who is an outstanding rider."

Mrs. Warren's voice was full of admiration as she finished:

"Her mother tells me that in Yorkshire she is acclaimed as the best woman equestrian anyone has ever seen."

Petula knew that Mrs. Warren liked praising the daughter of her friend. But to her every word was like a dagger striking at her heart.

How could she compete, she asked herself, with someone who fitted so admirably into the Duke's life?

Then she told herself severely that there was no question of a competition.

To her he was the magical enchantment which had transformed them for one ecstastic moment, but which could never be anything in their lives but a dream.

Immersed in her own unhappiness, she really paid no attention to the machinations of her uncle and all his plots and plans to marry her to the Earl of Temple Coombe.

The dinner-party to which he had invited them had not been the intimate affair which Sir Roderick was expecting.

Instead, thirty people had sat down to a long and tedious banquet, and they had been joined afterwards by a number of other guests who gambled for high stakes at the tables that were arranged in one of the Salons.

The majority of the gentlemen had been the age of their host, which Petula found with something approaching horror was, to her, very old indeed.

She had thought Lord Crowhurst an elderly man but the Earl was older still.

He had been distinguished-looking, if not handsome, in his youth, but now his face was lined, his hair was grey, and although he held himself erect she felt it was with somewhat of an effort.

Nevertheless, he was certainly not past the age of enjoying female company.

He flirted assiduously, Petula noticed, with the two beautiful women bedecked in jewels who sat on either side of him at dinner, and there was a look in his eye when he talked to her which made her feel embarrassed.

Just as her uncle had done, she thought he appraised her as if she were a horse, but it was different in that she knew he was considering her in a very different capacity and her whole being shrank from the idea of him even touching her.

To her delight, however, she learnt that the

Earl was leaving London the following day for Windsor Castle, where he was to stay for Ascot, and she was therefore reprieved from coming in contact with him again until his return.

There was no doubt that her uncle like a busy spider was spinning his web, and she felt as if she were a helpless little fly who had no chance of escape from the silken threads by which he was holding her captive.

Now Sir Roderick said almost harshly:

"If we cannot get Temple Coombe to say something definite by the end of next week, you will have to accept Crowhurst."

"Oh, no! Please . . . no, Uncle Roderick! Surely there could be . . . someone else . . . nicer than either of . . . them?"

"Nicer?" her uncle queried. "They are both extremely wealthy."

"B-but they are . . . old and I cannot bear to be . . . near either of them."

It was the first time that Petula had spoken in such a positive manner and her uncle looked at her in surprise.

"So you have some feelings after all?" he remarked.

"Of course I have feelings," Petula retorted, "but I am trying to behave as you wished me to do! Please . . . please do not make me marry either . . . Lord Crowhurst or the . . . Earl."

"And who are you hoping might take their place?" her uncle asked sarcastically. "The Prince of Wales? Or perhaps some Angel Gabriel whom we have not yet met? My dear Petula, let me make it clear once and for all that you cannot afford to be fastidious."

There was something in the way he spoke that made Petula look at him quickly.

"Have we spent . . . all the money you . . . obtained by selling the . . . Manor?" she asked.

"Things have proved more expensive than I

anticipated," her uncle answered, "and to tell the truth
I have had a bad run of luck at the tables."

"You have ... lost money?" she asked almost in
horror.

"Only a little. I have not risked much," her uncle
replied, "but even a little is too much where you and
I are concerned."

He walked across the room again before he said:

"The whole situation is difficult, as I might have
anticipated. Elaine cannot understand why I am
cheese-paring where you are concerned, and I dare
not tell her the truth."

"She loves you, Uncle Roderick."

"I know that," her uncle retorted, "but there is
nothing I can do about it."

For the first time Petula felt rather sorry for
him.

After all, he was in the same position as she was,
except that her situation was worse in that she had to
think of the man she loved being married to somebody else.

She was quite certain that Mrs. Warren would
never contemplate marriage with anyone except her
uncle.

She showed by the expression in her eyes and the
soft note in her voice how much she cared for him,
though she was very careful not to reveal it in any
other way.

"I shall be disappointed," Sir Roderick was saying, "if you have to settle for Crowhurst. He is an
excellent catch for someone like yourself. At the same
time, he is not in the same class as Temple Coombe."

"He is very ... old, Uncle Roderick."

For the first time since they had been talking,
her uncle smiled.

"Then you will be a widow, my dear, when you
are still comparatively young, with money to burn
and every fortune-hunter in the country at your feet."

Petula looked at him in a startled manner.

"It is then," Sir Roderick went on, "that you will

be able to be really kind to your poor uncle, who has done his best for you."

The whole idea made Petula feel not only disgusted but degraded.

It was bad enough to have to marry a man for his money, but to plan what would happen after he was dead was, she told herself, horrible.

She also felt her uncle was like a jailor incarcerating her in a golden prison from which she could never escape.

She thought how difficult it was going to be when she was married to keep giving him money, apart from the fact that sooner or later her husband would have to know she was not the heiress she had been acclaimed as being.

'I cannot bear it,' she thought.

She wanted to run away, to hide, to die if need be, rather than go on with this masquerade, which seemed to become more menacing, more frightening, day by day.

They went to Balls, to Receptions, to Assemblies, and Petula was taken to Almack's, which was the most formal and the most exclusive place at which to dance in the whole of the *Beau Monde.*

She was not invited to Carlton House, or if she was her uncle refused for her. He went there occasionally, she gathered, although not as frequently as he pretended.

At the end of each evening she knew that if she was truthful she had once again been looking for one face.

One face only in the crowds that glittered, chattered, gossipped, and seemed not only to look the same but to say the same day after day, night after night.

Then unexpectedly, when everything seemed miserable and dark with despair, she received a little basket of flowers.

It was very simple, very unpretentious, and when it was brought to her with several other floral

113

arrangements which had been left at Berkeley Square she hardly glanced at it.

Then she opened the card that was attached to the handle and the colour came into her pale face and she felt as if she had suddenly come alive.

The card contained only three words:

FROM MAJOR WOOD.

Could any code be more clear to her and more mysterious to anyone else?

He was thinking of her as she had been thinking of him, and the flowers when she looked at them told her everything she needed to know.

They were violets, white violets, and doubtless as the Season for them was over, they had been difficult to find.

But she remembered the small white violets in the wood peeping beneath the leaves and knew the Major had remembered them too.

Forgotten for the moment were her uncle's frightening plans, the old men she might have to marry, and her terror of the future.

All she could think of was that the Duke still loved her as she loved him.

This evening they were to go to the Opera and afterwards have an early night because, it being Saturday, there was no great Ball such as took place on other nights of the week.

Mrs. Warren had an explanation for this.

"Mrs. Fitzherbert is a Catholic," she said, "and does not approve of dancing on Sundays. It is not of course her opinion that matters directly, but she has persuaded the Prince not to accept any invitations to Balls given on Saturdays."

"It will be nice to get to bed early for once," Petula replied.

"That is what I should be saying, not you at your age!" Mrs. Warren laughed. "But I agree with you. However, it will be a worry because I am sure your uncle will gamble at one of his Clubs and it makes him so disagreeable if he loses."

Petula felt he had every reason to be disagreeable, but she did not say so, and they all three went and sat in a Box at Covent Garden.

To Petula the Opera was delightful but she was well aware that her uncle was bored.

Before the last act was half-finished he hurried them away because he said it would be difficult to find their carriage when everyone left at the same time.

They arrived back at Berkeley Square and the old Butler let them in, stifling a yawn as he did so.

"You need not stay up, Bruton," Sir Roderick said. "I will take the key with me, as I may be very late."

"You are going to White's?" Mrs. Warren asked with a little cry.

Sir Roderick nodded.

"I promised to meet some of my friends," he said evasively.

Petula was hardly listening.

There were two gifts of flowers standing on the table in the hall; one of them she realised at once came from Lord Crowhurst—she knew his handwriting by now—and the other was another small basket.

Quickly, in case her uncle should ask questions about it, she took the card from amongst the blooms and realised that it was enclosed in a sealed envelope.

As soon as her uncle had left, she hurried upstairs, hardly waiting to kiss Mrs. Warren good-night.

When she reached her own room she opened the envelope and found it contained just a line:

I AM WAITING FOR YOU IN CHARLES STREET.

She stared at it, feeling she could hardly believe what she read, then with her heart beating tumultuously she ran to the wardrobe.

115

She took down a dark cloak that she had brought with her from the country but which was far too dull and unfashionable to wear in London.

But it had a hood and she knew it was important that she should not be seen or recognised at this time of the night.

She pulled the hood over her head, draped the cloak over the white gown she wore, and tiptoed down the stairs.

As she expected, Bruton had hurried away to his own quarters. And at night Tomkins, the lady's-maid who served both her and Mrs. Warren, concentrated on the latter while Petula looked after herself.

In the hall there was only one candle burning in a silver sconce. The rest had been economically extinguished.

It took her only a second to open the door and slip outside.

Just for one moment she felt afraid because there were still many people walking about and carriages with splendidly attired servants driving past.

Keeping to the shade of the houses, she ran as swiftly as she dared towards Charles Street.

The carriage was there, the door was open, and she felt as though she flew into the inside of it like a bird seeking the security of its own nest.

Then the Duke's arms were round her and he was kissing her wildly, passionately, and possessively.

She was breathless, and at the insistence of his kisses she felt as if he awoke a fire within her to echo the fire on his lips and which she knew was smouldering in his eyes.

"I love you! I love you!" she wanted to say, but it was impossible to speak.

He held her so close that she knew that he had missed her as much as she had missed him.

The carriage drove away and once again stopped beside the Serpentine.

Now the water was not golden with sunshine but silver with the reflection of the stars.

"My precious, my life, my love!" the Duke said in an unsteady voice. "You are here—here in my arms after what has seemed a century of loneliness and agony without you."

"I ... I missed you ... too," Petula said, "but I should not be here ... only ... I had to come."

"And I had to see you. Oh, my darling, I had been so afraid that you would refuse and I should wait in vain."

"How did you know that we would be home early?" Petula asked.

She thought he smiled as he laid his cheek against her hair.

"I know everything you have done this past ghastly week," he said, "but I dared not try to see you until I was alone."

Petula knew then that Lady Emelye had gone back to Yorkshire.

"Everyone is talking of your beauty and of your admirers," the Duke said. "It has driven me nearly insane!"

"I have had to ... listen to ... everyone talking about ... you," Petula replied.

There was a little throb in her voice which told the Duke how much it had hurt her.

"My darling! How can either of us bear it?" he cried despairingly.

Then he was kissing her again, kissing her with the desperation of a man who sees everything he cares for slipping away from him.

"I love you!" he said at length. "I love you until it is impossible to think straight, but I know we cannot go on like this."

"You mean ... we must not ... see each other?"

"I mean," he said slowly, "that we must be brave. We have to go away together."

He felt Petula stiffen and he said:

"We will be married in France and not return to England until another scandal will prove more interesting than ours."

"B-but we cannot . . . we must not do that," Petula said in a low voice.

"I know what you are thinking, and I am thinking the same," the Duke answered. "But, my precious, just as you feel it impossible to marry another man, so I cannot marry anyone but you."

His arms tightened round her as he said:

"Even if you refuse to be my wife, I know that no other woman shall bear my name. It would be a sacrilege that I cannot contemplate and remain sane."

"But you are betrothed . . . you gave your . . . word," Petula murmured.

There was a little pause before the Duke said:

"I have thought it all out very clearly. Tomorrow I am going to Yorkshire to tell Emelye and her parents the truth. I intend to make them realise that I cannot and will not marry someone I do not love when my heart is elsewhere."

"They will be very . . . shocked."

"I am aware of that," the Duke answered, "and they will also think it an insult which might result in the Earl calling me out, but I think that unlikely."

Petula gave a little cry.

"If he did he might . . . kill you!"

"I am younger than he is and a far better shot!" the Duke said. "But I assure you the Earl will be well aware that that would cause an even greater scandal than the fact that I am refusing to marry his daughter."

He did not wait for Petula to answer but went on:

"Naturally I will give Emelye the opportunity to jilt me before I state categorically that, whether she does or does not, I intend to marry you."

"How can I . . . let you do . . . this?" Petula asked in a very small voice.

At the same time, something glorious and ecstatic was rising within her at the thought that he loved her so much that he would sacrifice his honour for her.

She knew it would be hard for him to go abroad

118.

for very long, to leave his estates, his horses, and the position he held not only in London but in the country.

As if he knew what she was thinking the Duke said:

"I must of course write to the King and ask him to relieve me of my duties at Court and in the County as his Lord Lieutenant."

"Am I . . . am I really . . . worth it?" Petula asked.

She turned her face up to his and in the faint light from the sky and the glow of the lanterns he could see the perfection of her features and her eyes looking up into his.

"For you," he said, "I would go down into hell, and that is where I am every moment when you are not with me."

There was a depth of sincerity in his voice that made Petula quiver. Then he said:

"I told you our love was different, my precious one, and that is exactly what it is. I love you, not only because you are the most beautiful person I have ever seen in my life, but because my heart is your heart and we are a part of each other so that when you are not there I am no longer a whole man."

"When you . . . are not there," Petula replied, "I find I cannot . . . think. I cannot see or hear . . . what is happening . . . round me."

"Then how can we let anything else matter?" the Duke asked simply. "Neither of us, my darling, can sentence ourselves to go through life maimed and crippled as we would be both mentally and spiritually without each other."

Petula made a little sound that was a sob but one of happiness.

She could hardly believe this was happening. She could hardly realise that after so much suffering she could really be with the Duke and their dream of love could become one of reality.

"I love you! I love . . . you!" she whispered.

Then the Duke was kissing her again until he

evoked something wild and wonderful within her so that she kissed him back and clung to him until a raging fire seemed to consume them both. . . .

*   *   *

"I worship you!" the Duke said much later. "And now, my precious love, I must take you home."

"I cannot . . . leave you," Petula murmured.

"Soon we will be together every moment of the day and night," he said. "We will go to France and then to Italy. There are so many things I want to show you now that the war is over."

"I am . . . afraid that you will miss . . ." Petula began, but he interrupted her.

"I will miss nothing and nobody as long as I have you. That is all I want—to be with you, to love you, and to teach you to love me."

"I do love you already!"

"Not as much as I intend you will in the future," the Duke answered.

He kissed her forehead before he said:

"You are so sweet, so pure, and so innocent that I can imagine nothing more perfect or more absorbing than to teach you, my lovely one, about love."

"S-suppose after all you give up for me . . . I disappoint you?" Petula asked.

"I may disappoint you," he answered.

"You will never do that," she said quickly. "You are so . . . magnificent and so . . . wonderful that there is not a man in the whole world like . . . you, nor will there . . . ever be one!"

The Duke held her very close against him. Then he said:

"Shall we walk for a moment under the trees and remind ourselves of the place where I first kissed you, when I knew that you were what I had sought and never found, and everything I really wanted in life?"

"Please . . . let us do . . . that."

The Duke opened the door and before Jason could jump from the box to hold it for them he had helped Petula out.

It was cool and very quiet under the trees, and when they were out of sight of the carriage they stood beneath the branches with the silvery water at their feet and the Duke put his arms round Petula.

He could just see the loveliness of her face as she lifted it to his. He could feel the softness of her body as it melted against him and the passionate beating of her heart.

For a moment he did not kiss her, he only looked down at her. Then he said:

"I pledge myself to make you happy, and to ensure that our love is greater and more tremendous than anything in the whole world, or indeed in Heaven itself!"

Petula drew in her breath, then she replied very softly:

"I will . . . try to make your . . . sacrifice for me . . . worthwhile, and I shall . . . live for you and love you with my . . . heart, my . . . soul and my . . . mind. I have . . . nothing else to . . . give you."

"Do you think I want anything else?" he asked, then once again he was kissing her.

It seemed to Petula as if there was something sacred and holy now in their kiss. It was almost as if they had taken their vows at the altar and received the blessing of God.

She felt as if he carried her up into the stars above them and that they were joined as one by the Divine Power that is life itself.

Then with the Duke's arm round her they walked back slowly and in silence towards the carriage, both feeling at peace and as if they had reached harbour after passing through tumultuous and dangerous seas.

"I shall leave for Yorkshire tomorrow," the Duke said as the carriage drove off. "They are not expecting me until next week, but I dare not leave you alone for very much longer because of what your uncle is planning for you."

"Nothing will ... matter as long as you ... come back to me," Petula said.

"Just play for time," the Duke advised. "You will understand, my darling, that I cannot talk to Sir Roderick until I have told Emelye what I intend to do."

"Will she be ... very upset?"

The Duke seemed to consider this question for a moment.

"I do not think so," he said. "She is not in love with me as you and I are in love, but I think she is fond of me—after all, we have known each other for so many years."

"It will be ... difficult to ... hurt her."

"I have no choice," the Duke answered. "Either I hurt her, or you and myself."

"I understand ... as long as you will never ... regret it afterwards."

"Never! Never! Never!" he said, and the last word was spoken against her lips.

The carriage stopped once again at the corner of Charles Street and when Jason got down the Duke said:

"Drive to the front door of Forty-seven Berkeley Square."

"Very good, Your Grace."

Jason shut the door and as Petula stared wide-eyed the Duke said:

"I am through with pretence! I am through with hiding and sending you anonymous little baskets of flowers when really what I want to give you is the moon, the stars, and the sun to express my love."

Petula understood what he was saying. At the same time, she hoped that her uncle by some unfortunate mischance was not returning at the same time that she was.

Then belatedly, because she was so bemused by what was happening, she said:

"I have just remembered . . . I cannot get in through the front door. . . . After all you will have to take me to the Mews."

The Duke gave a short laugh.

"So much for my grandiose gesture! Never mind, when I return we will both use the front door together, hand in hand."

Jason was told to go round to the Mews and the carriage took them there.

The place was in darkness but the doors were open and Petula knew that her uncle had not returned.

The Duke kissed both of her hands, then her lips.

"I shall be away for six days, my darling," he said, "and then you can leave everything to me. I will look after you and you will never have to worry about anything again."

Petula laid her cheek against his hand as he held hers, before as the door of the carriage opened she stepped out.

She did not look back, but just hurried into the darkness of the stables and along the passage which led to the house.

When she reached her own room she threw herself down on the bed, trying to think, trying to realise what this would mean.

"I shall . . . belong to him, I shall be his . . . wife!" she told herself. "Oh, God, how grateful I am!"

She lay for some time just as she was.

Then she pulled off her cloak and without waiting to undress knelt beside the bed to say a prayer of thanksgiving that God had blessed her in a manner she had never imagined possible.

❖   ❖   ❖

Petula awoke knowing that she had slept for only a few hours.

123

She had fallen asleep feeling that the Duke's arms were round her and his lips were on hers.

She thought the sunshine glinting through the sides of the curtains was more golden than it had ever been before.

The room seemed to be filled with the fragrance of flowers and the music which came from her own heart.

"Six days! Only six days!" she said, and knew that every minute that passed drew her closer to the moment when she would be with the Duke.

There was a knock on the door and Tomkins came in.

She drew back the curtains before she said:

"I've called you much earlier than usual, Miss, as there's a note arrived for you a few minutes ago and the groom said 'twas of the utmost urgency and should be given to you immediately!"

Petula sat up in bed and put out her hand eagerly to take the note.

There was no need to guess from whom it came, and there was a look of radiance on her face which caused Tomkins to look at her curiously as she opened the envelope.

She saw that it contained two pages.

On one was written:

My dearest, most beloved:
What else can I do?

For a moment Petula felt she could not open the other piece of paper, and when she did so she saw the engraved address at the top of it and felt as if it swam in front of her eyes. It read:

Kirkby Hall,
Yorkshire

My dear Adrian,
I am writing this and sending it post-

haste to London to ask you to come here with all possible speed. Emelye went riding this morning immediately after her arrival and had a very bad fall.

The Doctors think she may have broken her back, which means she may be paralysed. She is asking for you and I can only beg of you to reach us without a moment's delay. I have sent to Windsor for her mother.

All it remains to say is that I am heartbroken at what has occurred—an accident which is quite inexplicable.

Yours,
Kirkby

Petula read it through twice and the second time she felt as though the letter itself were covered in darkness.

She had thanked God too prematurely. She had grasped at her happiness and now it had eluded her.

From a long way away she heard Tomkins say:

"You look as though you've had a shock, Miss. Is there anything I can do for you?"

"No . . . nothing," Petula answered.

That was the answer. There was nothing anyone could do!

Without really being conscious of her movements, Petula dressed and only as she walked downstairs did she realise it was only a little after six-thirty.

Vaguely at the back of her mind she thought of writing a letter to the Duke, then she knew there was no point in it and anyway he would have already left for Yorkshire.

She went into the Library, hardly seeing her surroundings, conscious only of a pain that seemed to grow and grow in intensity until it filled not only her whole being but the world, and there was nothing but pain.

Then, so suddenly that it made her start, the door was opened and her uncle stood there.

She looked at him and thought for a moment that he must have had an accident.

There was an expression she did not understand on his face, his white cravat was a limp rag round his throat, and he held in both hands his high-crowned hat.

"Petula!" he said in a voice that was so hoarse it was little more than a croak. "I am brilliant! I am a genius! You see before you a man who—possesses a —fortune!"

Petula stared at him incredulously, then slowly he tipped up his hat and a shower of gold coins, notes of hand, and cheques fell from it to the floor.

"Twenty thousand pounds at least! A fortune!" Sir Roderick cried. "A fortune—Petula!"

He swayed as he stood there and Petula ran to his side to take his arm.

"You are ill, Uncle Roderick."

"Not ill—drunk!" he replied. "Drunk with joy and the thought that never again need I touch a— damned card!"

She helped him to a chair and he sprawled in it, his legs outstretched.

"A fortune!" he repeated beneath his breath, his words slightly slurred. "I am a—rich man!"

Petula stood looking at him for a moment, then at the carpet, bestrewn with money. Turning, she ran up the stairs to Mrs. Warren's room.

She entered the room without knocking and hurried across it to draw back the curtains.

As the sunshine came flooding in she turned round to see Mrs. Warren sitting up in bed, staring at her with startled eyes.

"It is Uncle Roderick," Petula said breathlessly at the speed at which she had run. "He needs you! Come downstairs to him."

"There has not been an accident?" Mrs. Warren cried.

Even as she spoke she began to get out of bed.

"There has been no accident, but he will tell you what has happened," Petula answered.

Mrs. Warren was looking very attractive in a little lace-trimmed muslin cap that she always wore over her hair at night.

Petula picked up her robe, also trimmed with lace, which lay over a chair, and helped her into it.

"Hurry!" she said. "He is in the Library and will want to tell you himself what has occurred."

"I do hope it is nothing disastrous," Mrs. Warren murmured in an anxious voice.

Then, spurred by Petula's air of urgency, she slipped her feet into her soft slippers and, still buttoning her robe, began to walk down the corridor towards the stairs.

Sir Roderick was lying in the chair where Petula had left him, but now his eyes were closed and she knew he had fallen asleep from drink and exhaustion.

Mrs. Warren stepped over the money without really noticing it and went to Sir Roderick to kneel down beside him.

"Roderick!" she called. "Roderick!"

It seemed as if her voice awoke him, but he only opened his eyes to say again in an incoherent voice:

"I—am a—rich man!"

"He has been gambling all night," Petula explained. "He only arrived home a few minutes ago."

Mrs. Warren looked for the first time at the money scattered on the carpet.

"He has . . . won all . . . that?" she asked in an incredulous tone.

"So he told me," Petula replied.

Mrs. Warren rose a little uncertainly to her feet.

"Is it . . . possible?" she whispered.

"It is not only possible, but it means, dearest Mrs. Warren, that now you can be married and you can look after him."

She put her arms round the older woman and

127

kissed her, thinking as she did so that no-one would ever say the same words to her.

She felt the tears come into her eyes and said hastily:

"Will you look after Uncle Roderick?"

Without waiting for an answer, she went from the room, shutting the door behind her.

She ran upstairs and rang the bell.

When Tomkins appeared she said to her:

"Will you please pack my trunk for me? I cannot take everything, but perhaps the rest can follow later."

"You are going away, Miss?"

"Yes," Petula answered resolutely, "I am going away."

As Tomkins began packing she changed into a gown she thought suitable for travelling.

Then she took down from the wardrobe the dark cloak she had worn when she had gone with the Duke into the park at night.

It brought back memories that she hastily pushed aside to choose the plainest of her bonnets, knowing that most of them would attract a great deal of comment and speculation amongst the travellers in a stage-coach.

"We'll have to get another trunk, Miss," Tomkins said.

"This trunk will be enough for now," Petula replied. "My evening-gowns and my bonnets can stay here. I will not need them."

"Not need them?" Tomkins repeated in surprise, but Petula did not enlighten her as to why they would be unnecessary.

Instead, picking up her gloves and a handbag, she went downstairs again, spoke to Bruton, who was in the hall, and then went into the Library.

Her uncle was still asleep but Mrs. Warren was sitting at the desk, counting the money she had collected from the floor.

She looked up as Petula entered and said in an awe-struck voice:

"Twenty-one thousand five hundred pounds! I can not believe it!"

"Uncle Roderick said he would never touch a card again, and that is a promise that you must make him keep."

A faint smile touched Mrs. Warren's lips.

"He never really enjoyed gambling."

Petula looked at the piles of gold guineas in front of her and asked:

"Will you give me one hundred pounds and tell Uncle Roderick when he wakes that I asked for it?"

Mrs. Warren looked at her with a question in her eyes and Petula explained:

"I am going away. Uncle Roderick will explain to you that I am not the heiress I pretended to be, but now I am . . . free."

"My dearest child . . ." Mrs. Warren expostulated, but Petula held up her hand.

"I would rather Uncle Roderick told you everything," she said, "and as I want to avoid arguments and since also I am sure he would prefer to be alone with you, I want to leave before he wakes."

"Then take anything you want," Mrs. Warren said with a little gesture of her hand towards the piles of money.

Petula selected eight ten-pound notes and picked up ten guineas which she required for her journey. She put it all in her handbag, then said.

"If we never meet again, I want to thank you for all your kindness to me and for introducing me to the Social World."

She kissed Mrs. Warren as she spoke, but did not wait to answer all the questions she saw hovering on her lips.

She merely walked out of the room, closing the door behind her.

Her trunk was already in the hall and Bruton had, on her instructions, called a hackney carriage.

He and the coachman lifted the trunk onto the front of it and Petula got in behind.

Barbara Cartland

"Good-bye, Bruton," she said to the Butler. "I think Sir Roderick and Mrs. Warren would like you to take some black coffee to the Library."

"Very good, Miss," the Butler answered. "And I hopes you has a good journey."

"Thank you," Petula answered. "Will you instruct the coachman to go to the Two-Necked Swan in Islington?"

Bruton shouted the words to the coachman, who appeared to be rather deaf. Then he whipped up his tired horse and they started to move through Berkeley Square.

Petula remembered how the Duke had proposed to drive to the front door of number 47, saying:

"I am through with pretence. I am through with hiding!"

He had spoken too quickly, she thought, and it was perhaps prophetic that after what he had called his "grandiose gesture" he had had, after all, to take her round to the back to the Mews.

She remembered how he had laughed and said:

"When I return we will both use the front door together, hand in hand."

Now that would never happen!

He would be tied to Emelye not only legally but morally, in a way which Petula knew would preclude them even from seeing each other secretly.

Could they feel anything but guilt if they deceived a woman who was paralysed and could therefore not compete for his affections?

This was the end.

By a twist and turn of fate, at the very last moment her happiness had been snatched away from her, leaving only the utter darkness of despair, without even a ray of hope.

Chapter Seven

It took Petula nearly five days to reach Buckden and the journey was excessively uncomfortable in hot, crowded stage-coaches.

Passengers received little or no attention at the Posting Inns at which they stopped and only the cheapest and most uncomfortable rooms were assigned them where they stayed each night.

Eventually she reached the nearest hamlet on the main highway to Buckden and there she had to wait for a carrier to convey her the last four miles to the village.

When she drove down the dusty lane and had her first sight of the little grey stone Church where her father and mother were buried in the Churchyard, she knew that nothing had changed since she went away, but for the rest of her life it would never be the same.

It was as if she had been ship-wrecked and in the traumatic experience had lost so much of her original self that she was now a different person altogether.

The carrier, whom she knew because he had been coming to the village ever since her childhood, drew up outside Honeysuckle Cottage and Petula saw that since she had seen it last the garden had been tidied and was bright with flowers.

She opened the latch-gate and walked down the small path bordered by pinks.

Even as she reached the door it opened and Annie stood there.

"Miss Petula!" she exclaimed. "I couldn't believe my very eyes when I saw you through the window!"

"I have come home, Annie," Petula said with a little break in her voice.

The carrier carried in her trunk and Petula pulled off her bonnet and looked round the small Sitting-Room.

It was filled with all the special pieces of furniture and little treasures that her mother had accumulated and loved.

There were ornaments of little or no intrinsic value, but to Petula they were part of her childhood and part too, she thought, of the future that remained to her.

She paid the carrier and he thanked her for a generous tip and touched his forelock.

"You gave him too much, Miss Petula," Annie said in the scolding voice she knew so well. "Have you come into a fortune all of a sudden?"

"All the money we have in the world is in this bag," Petula answered as she set it down on the table. "It will have to last us, Annie, for a long time."

She spoke in such a strange voice that instantly Annie went to her.

"What's the matter? What's happened to you, dearie?" she enquired.

There was so much solicitude and the gentleness she had known as a child in Annie's words that Petula burst into tears.

* * *

The Duke, driving towards Yorkshire, felt a despair that he knew Petula too must be feeling.

The letter had come out of the blue, and he knew that it destroyed all his plans of happiness for the future in a way nothing else could have done.

If Emelye was paralysed from a fall out riding—

and he knew exactly what that meant—it would be impossible for him to refuse to marry her.

Doubtless out of consideration she would offer to release him from his promise, but only an outsider, a man with no principles whatsoever, would throw over the woman to whom he was engaged to be married because she was incapacitated.

It might have put paid to his happiness, it might mean that he could never have an heir to succeed him. But the code by which a gentleman lived and was recognised laid down that his behaviour in such circumstances must be chivalrous and beyond reproach.

Only by driving at a speed which required every ounce of his concentration did the Duke prevent himself from crying aloud at his own despair and unhappiness.

The Countess of Kirkby had been commanded to stay at Windsor in attendance on the Queen, and as she was an hereditary Lady of the Bedchamber it was impossible for her to refuse.

The Earl and Emelye had therefore left for Yorkshire together and the Duke had been aware that Emelye was longing to get back to her horses.

"I have two in training which are going to be superlative," she said to him. "I told Edward Trafford to raise the jumps while I was away, after which I am quite certain they will be capable of going round the Grand National course with the greatest of ease."

The Duke knew that Trafford was her father's steeple-chase trainer and had a big reputation in the racing world.

He had, however, said:

"Be careful, Emelye. Those sort of jumps are hard enough for a man, let alone a woman."

"You might say that to most women," Emelye replied, "but not to me."

The Duke had smiled.

"No. You are certainly exceptional. At the same time, very high jumps can be dangerous, as we both know."

He was thinking that one of the Earl's horses had broken a leg the previous year in one of the classic steeple-chases and had had to be destroyed.

As if she deliberately put his warning out of her mind, Emelye had gone on to talk of the horses she was training. There were some foals that had been born to a very expensive thoroughbred mare which the Earl had purchased three years ago.

"You will have to improve your stable, Adrian," she said teasingly, "and of course once we are married I will help you."

"Thank you," the Duke had replied sarcastically.

His horses had won more races and were considered on the whole to be of far better stock than the Earl's.

As the Duke expected to be travelling to Yorkshire fairly frequently, he had already sent his own horses to every important Posting Inn and he therefore reached Kirkby Castle in record time.

As he drew his sweating team to a standstill the Earl came hurrying down the steps from the front door, saying:

"I did not expect you so soon, Adrian, but it is good of you to arrive so quickly.

"How is Emelye?" the Duke asked.

He was hot, rather tired and would have liked to have a bath but he knew there was no chance of that.

"I promised to take you to her right away," the Earl answered. "She has asked for no-one else ever since the accident."

"What happened?" the Duke asked as they started to climb the staircase.

"She insisted on having one jump raised even higher than Trafford advised. Even so, it was a mystery how she managed to fall in the way she did. The horse hardly grazed his knees."

134

The Duke did not reply and they walked along the corridor in silence.

The Earl knocked softly on a door and it was opened by the Countess, looking very drawn and lined. She held out both her hands.

"Adrian! Thank God you are here! I only arrived this morning, to find Emelye asking for you, and she will not rest until she has seen you."

"How is she?" the Duke asked automatically.

The Countess's lips moved silently and the tears came into her eyes so that there was no need for words.

The Duke walked past her into the dimly lit room and moved towards the bed. Emelye was lying very still in the centre of it and her eyes were closed.

"Emelye!" he called in a low voice.

Her eyes opened slowly and he thought they focussed on him with difficulty. Then there was a faint smile on her lips.

The Duke took her hand in his.

"I am sorry."

"Are . . . we . . . alone?"

She had difficulty in saying the words and though they were low he could hear her clearly.

He glanced towards the door, which the Countess had shut behind him.

"Quite alone."

"Then . . . listen . . . Adrian. I have . . . something to . . . ask you."

"You know I will do anything you want."

"I . . . am . . . going to . . . die."

"No, of course not . . ." he began.

"Do not . . . argue with . . . me," she said, "just . . . listen. I have . . . not long."

The Duke held her hand and waited.

"I want you . . . to give Edward enough . . . money to get to . . . America. He must . . . get away . . . but he . . . cannot afford . . . to go unless . . . you help him."

"Edward Trafford?" the Duke questioned, bewildered.

"Yes, Edw-ard . . ." Emelye said. "He . . . cannot stay here."

"What are you saying to me?" the Duke asked.

"I . . . meant to . . . fall," Emelye said. "It was not . . . the horse's fault. I meant . . . to kill . . . myself."

"But why, Emelye? Why?" the Duke asked.

"I am . . . having . . . Edward's baby. The Doctor has . . . promised not to . . . tell Papa and . . . Mama until I am . . . dead. Then . . . he says he . . . must do so."

The Duke was silent from sheer surprise. Emelye went on in a slightly weaker voice:

"There is no-one . . . I can ask but . . . you. Promise me . . . you will help Edward . . . I have loved him . . . ever since I was a . . . child when he . . . first taught me to . . . ride."

Her voice almost faded away on the last words and the Duke said:

"I promise you. I will give him the money to leave the country."

"And . . . enough . . . to start . . . again in . . . America?"

"All he needs," the Duke answered.

Emelye gave a sigh.

"Thank you . . . Adrian. I know . . . I have been . . . a fool . . . but it was . . . worth it. We were . . . so happy until . . . Papa said I had to . . . marry you."

The Duke lifted her hand to his lips. Then she said:

"Tell . . . Edward they will not . . . let me see him but tell him . . . I am not . . . afraid to die . . . and . . . I love him!"

"I will tell him."

Emelye shut her eyes and he felt that, as if now she had accomplished what she wanted, she was drifting away—deliberately letting go of life.

"Emelye!" the Duke said insistently. "Emelye!"

But her hand was limp in his, and although she was still breathing he knew without being told that she would not live long.

He rose from the bed and went to the door to call her father and mother into the room. . . .

❋ ❋ ❋

Petula, tidying away the cups and saucers after she and Annie had finished their tea, carried them into the small kitchen and put them down in the sink.

Everything was exceedingly neat and tidy and the cottage made her feel as if she were living in a doll's house.

It seemed so minute after Berkeley Square and the rambling dilapidated Manor. And because Annie had squeezed so many things into the small rooms, Petula felt that sometimes she was as large as a giantess in a Lilliputian land.

She found in the cottage not only the things she had given Annie but that a large number of other bits and pieces from the Manor were there as well.

"Mr. Barrowick threw them out, if you can believe it," Annie said. "He told Adam, whom he's taken into his employment with a lot of others from the village, to burn them! Did you ever hear of such vandalism?"

Petula found it hard not to laugh at the indignation in Annie's voice, but when she went upstairs she did in fact laugh, even though the traces of tears were still on her cheeks.

One of the things which Mr. Barrowick had not considered good enough for himself was the big four-poster bed in which her father had always slept as had generations of previous Buckdens.

Annie had placed it in the largest of the bedrooms and it left practically no room for anything else.

"Oh, Annie, how could you have that here?" Petula exclaimed.

"It was the master's bed and it wasn't right that anyone else should have it," Annie said stoutly.

"How on earth did you get it up the stairs?"

"Adam carved it into pieces, then he and Ned put them together again."

They had made a good job of it, Petula had to admit.

At the same time, it seemed ridiculous that the best and largest bed-room in Honeysuckle Cottage should be filled with a carved four-poster with ancient red curtains on which was emblazoned the Buckden coat-of-arms.

Although it was faded and frayed it still seemed, Petula thought, to have a pride about it which she told herself she must emulate.

Annie had of course insisted that she should sleep on her father's bed, and inevitably the person she thought of in the long dark hours of the night was the man who had used it last.

She would lie, pretending that the Duke's arms were round her and his lips were on hers.

Then, because she yearned and ached for him, she would find herself crying helplessly and miserably until from sheer exhaustion she fell asleep.

As she dried the saucers and put them on the shelf Annie said:

"I'm just going to slip out and get something for dinner. Is there anything you fancy, dearie?"

"I . . . I am not . . . hungry."

"You'll eat even if I have to stand over you and make you do it," Annie snapped. "It's so thin you're getting, I'll be asking the new Doctor one of these days to come and see what's wrong with you."

"There is nothing . . . wrong with me," Petula replied. "I am just . . . not hungry."

Annie's lips tightened, which meant, Petula knew, that she would spend more money than was necessary in trying to tempt her to food.

She knew there was no use arguing with Annie even while she resented the money Annie would insist on spending, knowing that even a hundred pounds would not last forever.

She had not heard from her uncle since she had left London and she wondered if he was angry at her for leaving. However, she felt he would in fact be relieved, now that he had plenty of money himself.

If she was truthful she was not worrying about receiving a letter from her uncle but hoping against hope that there would be one from the Duke.

"If he does write to me here it will be to London," she told herself. "But there is nothing either of us can say to the other, so why do I go on longing to hear from him?"

She heard the cottage door shut behind Annie and she suddenly wanted to go to the little wood.

The idea had been in her mind ever since she returned to Buckden, but she had known that it would be so agonising to recapture the magic of that first kiss that she had forced herself to stay in the cottage.

She had learnt from both Annie and Adam that the Manor itself was a hive of activity.

Mr. Barrowick had brought in an army of builders, carpenters, and stone-masons to restore the house to its original glory.

"He fancies he's the Prince of Wales and is a-spending money like water," Annie said scornfully.

Petula had learnt that most of the people in the village thought it extremely presumptuous that Mr. Barrowick should try to take the place of her father.

She knew, as it was getting late in the afternoon, that the workmen who had come some distance to the village would have gone home and it would therefore be safe for her to walk without being seen across the lawn and down the field to the little wood.

Without bothering to put on her bonnet, because there was a path winding at the back of the village into the shrubberies, Petula found her way and saw that the gardens which had grown so wild were already being trimmed into shape.

The lawns had been cut and she had learnt from Adam that they were to be extended right down to the edge of the wood itself.

139

The field was still a little rough but Petula thought only of reaching the shadow of the birch trees. Yet when she reached them they seemed to swim before her eyes.

The violets had gone and so had the primroses and the blue-bells. The leaves were thicker on the trees, but still the sun percolated golden through them to make a pattern on the ground beneath them.

Now it was the evening sun, lacking the pale shining gold of the sun which had shone so brilliantly in the early morning when she had seen the Major coming towards her between the trunks of the trees.

She stood for a moment feeling the sensations and emotions she had known then sweep over her like a tidal wave.

Then there had been the magical enchantment, but now it had deepened and intensified until her whole being throbbed not only at the memory of it but because it was lost.

"Oh, God, help me to ... forget!" she prayed suddenly.

Then her tears blinded her so that she could no longer see the sunshine.

* * *

The funeral was over and the Duke knew that now there was nothing to keep him at the Castle.

Emelye had been laid to rest in a Church-yard at the end of the park, and because the Earl and Countess were so heart-broken it had been a very quiet ceremony, with only a few close friends and relations and those who worked on the estate present.

Before it took place, however, the Duke had been very busy.

He had not only given Edward Trafford the money he had promised Emelye he would, but he had also arranged for his passage to America and given him introductions to various owners and breeders when he arrived there.

"I don't know why you should do this for me, M'Lord," Trafford had said.

"I do not intend to discuss it with you," the Duke answered. "All I am concerned with is keeping any knowledge of it from the Earl and Countess."

He spoke coldly because he considered that Trafford, who was a much older man, had behaved extremely reprehensibly towards a young girl while he was in the Earl's employment.

He told himself however that he had at the moment no wish to censure anyone, but only to make everything pass off as smoothly as Emelye would have wished.

He had had a difficult time with the Doctor, who considered it his duty to inform the Earl and Countess of the real reason for their daughter's death.

The Duke had used all his persuasive powers.

The real difficulty lay in the fact that the Doctor was a good, straight-forward man who was extremely shocked at what had occurred.

Finally, after nearly an hour's argument, the Doctor had capitulated and given the Duke his word of honour that he would never divulge to anyone Emelye's condition when she died.

Now the Duke knew that his part in the proceedings was over and he would no longer have to pretend, which had been exceedingly difficult, that he himself was very upset.

The Earl came into the room and the Duke said:

"I think now that you and your wife would wish to be alone. So, I have given orders for my things to be packed and my Phaeton to be brought round to the door."

"You are leaving us?" the Earl exclaimed.

The Duke nodded, with difficulty restrained the Earl from making a speech of gratitude, and managed to leave without saying good-bye to the Countess, who he knew after the funeral would be weeping in her bed-room.

As he drove away down the drive with Jason beside him he felt as if a burden had fallen from his shoulders and for the first time he was free to think about himself.

"The travelling landau's gone ahead of us, Your Grace," Jason said. "They asked where you'd be staying tonight and I says as I thought it would be at that Inn near Huntingford."

"Yes, that will do," the Duke replied absent-mindedly, "though we need not change horses there."

"No, Your Grace. When we stops for luncheon tomorrow will be soon enough for that."

Suddenly the Duke remembered that Huntingford was not far from Buckden and it was in fact the Inn to which Petula had referred when he had asked where he could stay.

He had a sudden feeling that he must go to Buckden, to look at the place where he had met her first. Some undefinable instinct within him made him feel he should go there not only to reminisce but for some other reason.

He told himself that now that the evenings were light until eleven o'clock or later, he would have plenty of time to visit Buckden, then get back to Huntingford before it was dark.

While the Duke preferred to travel in his Phaeton, his valet and any other servants who were necessary went ahead of him in a travelling landau, carrying besides themselves a multitudinous pile of luggage.

It ensured his comfort in that when he arrived at an Inn everything he needed had been unpacked, the bed had been remade with his own linen, his dinner had been ordered, and the wine he was likely to prefer had been brought up from the cellars.

He accepted such luxury automatically now that he had inherited the Dukedom, but because he had been a soldier he was, as he had told Petula, quite ready when it was necessary to rough it.

There was however no need now for that, and

tonight, even if he wished to do so, he would not be able to sleep in the dilapidated Manor, because it no longer belonged to the Buckdens.

He could understand Petula resenting, although they had never had time to talk about it, her uncle selling the house and the estate which had been in their family for so many years.

But he told himself that once they were married she would have so many magnificent houses in which to be the Chatelaine that she would never regret her old home.

At the same time, he wanted to go to Buckden.

"I am being sentimental," he told himself, and knew that was a very mild way to express his feelings where Petula was concerned.

Jason was surprised when they turned off the main highway about five o'clock and started down the twisting lane which led to the village where they had had an accident.

"We be going to Buckden, Your Grace?" the groom asked after a moment.

"Yes," the Duke replied.

He volunteered no further information and they drove in silence until the small grey Church with its pointed spire came in sight.

Then as the Duke drove his team more slowly Jason gave an exclamation.

"There's the Nurse to Miss Petula, Your Grace," he said, "who looked after us when we stayed at th' Manor that night."

The Duke looked where he pointed.

There was no mistaking Annie in her neat black bonnet, and despite the heat wearing a grey woollen shawl over her grey gown.

The Duke drew the Phaeton to a standstill beside her and she stared at him in surprise.

"Why, it's Major Chester!" she exclaimed. "Fancy seeing you again, Sir."

"I have not forgotten how kind and hospitable

143

you were to us when we came to the Manor," the Duke replied.

"I can't be offering hospitality there any more, Sir," Annie answered. "It's been sold and I'm living now just here in Honeysuckle Cottage."

The Duke saw that he had drawn up his horses almost opposite a small thatched cottage standing by itself, its porch covered with honeysuckle.

"It certainly looks very attractive and worthy of its name," he remarked.

"It's small, but comfortable," Annie said.

She hesitated, then added:

"If you'd be liking a little refreshment, Sir, I'm sure Miss Petula would be pleased to see you."

The Duke started so that for a moment his hand on the reins tightened. Then he said:

"Is Miss Petula here?"

"Yes, Sir. She came back from London some days ago, and judging by her appearance it did her no good!"

The Duke handed the reins to Jason.

"I shall be very glad to avail myself of your offer," he said to Annie, and got down from the Phaeton.

* * *

Petula fought against giving way to her tears.

What was the point, she asked herself, of crying when she should really be grateful for having known a happiness which she was sure was accorded to few people?

She was ashamed for having wept so bitterly every night, yet it was impossible to deny the yearning of her whole body for the man she loved and who she knew loved her.

Perhaps, she thought, it would have been better if he did not care rather than to know that this terrible gulf between them, a gulf it was impossible to bridge, existed.

"I must be brave," she said, "and I will not come here again."

She must have been in the wood for a long time and she thought she would take one last look at the beauty of it.

Then it would be etched forever in her mind and she would remember it only when she was brave enough to think of the love and the wonder she had found there.

She pulled out her handkerchief, and wiping her eyes almost fiercely started to retrace her steps back to Annie and the cottage.

Suddenly she thought she must be dreaming.

Someone was coming towards her through the trees and she imagined for one wild moment that she had stepped back in time and was seeing what had happened before, seeing it so clearly, so vividly, that he was almost real.

Then as the Duke came nearer she knew he was real!

For a moment she could only stand looking at him as if she had been turned to stone, then with a little cry which seemed to echo amongst the trees she ran towards him.

She flung herself against him and as his arms went round her it was impossible even to ask why he was there or what was happening.

His lips came down on hers and she could think of nothing but the wonder of his kiss and the rapture that swept through her like a shaft of sunlight.

He was with her, she was close to him, and he was drawing her heart, as he had done before, from between her lips, and she was his. His completely and absolutely, and it was impossible to think of anything else.

The Duke held her closer and still closer and somewhere in the depths of her soul Petula prayed that she might die because she had never known such happiness and perhaps it would never come again.

At last the Duke raised his head and looked down at her.

At her mouth, soft from his kisses, at her eyes

145

misty with tears looking up into his, at her cheeks, pale from the intensity of the feelings which made her whole body tremble against his.

"My precious! My darling!" he said. "I have found you again, and everything is all right!"

He saw her eyes widen and said:

"We can be together and now nothing in the whole world can prevent it."

Petula gave a little cry of sheer happiness, then the Duke was kissing her again.

He kissed her until the wood swam dizzily round her and she felt as if the sunshine was so blinding that she could no longer see. But it became a part of them both so that they glowed with a spiritual light.

"I love you! Oh, Adrian . . . I love . . . you!" she whispered, "and I thought I should . . . never see you . . . again."

"Not only will you see me, but you will be with me always and forever, my darling," the Duke said. "We are to be married this evening, so perhaps we had better go back to the cottage."

"M-married?"

Petula could hardly breathe the word.

"I have spoken to the Vicar, who told me he had known you since you were a baby. I have explained to him because I am in mourning our marriage has to be quiet and a secret, and he has agreed that no-one shall know of it except your Nurse."

"Oh . . . Adrian!"

Petula could hardly speak or breathe.

"You will understand the need for secrecy when I tell you that Emelye is dead," the Duke said.

Petula was still.

"The fall . . . killed her?"

"Yes, it killed her."

"It must have been very . . . upsetting for you."

"She told me before she died that she loved someone else," the Duke said. "That knowledge, my precious one, as you will understand now, set me free—

free from the prickings of conscience or any feelings of guilt."

He had told himself as he drove away from Kirkby Castle that that was all the story Petula need ever know.

Now he felt her give a deep sigh as if she also felt free and absolved from any qualms of disloyalty.

"We are . . . really to be . . . married?" she asked.

The Duke's arms tightened about her.

"Do you think I can risk waiting any longer to make you mine before something else prevents you from becoming my wife?"

"How . . . did you know I was . . . here?"

"I must have felt it in my bones," the Duke answered. "And I might ask you the same question."

Petula smiled.

"The morning after I received your letter," she said, "Uncle Roderick came back from the Club, having won over twenty-one thousand pounds."

"So you came home, my precious."

She had known he would understand and she said simply:

"There was no reason for me to stay."

"No, of course not," the Duke answered, "and I am grateful, darling, that my instinct where you are concerned has saved me many days of driving. I was on my way to London to find you."

"Perhaps it was Fate that brought us together again, as it did in the first place," Petula said.

"If it was Fate, then it has given us some uncomfortable moments," the Duke said dryly. "But now all its twists and turns with our love are over, and once you are my wife I am prepared to defy the Heavens themselves to keep us apart."

He kissed her again, then with his arm round her they walked back towards Honeysuckle Cottage.

*   *   *

The sun had sunk and in the dusky sky the first stars were coming out as Petula and the Duke moved into the tiny Sitting-Room of the cottage.

It was so small and low-ceilinged that it made the Duke look almost abnormally tall, and yet so attractive and elegant that Petula instinctively moved towards him, knowing from the expression in his eyes that he was waiting for her to do so.

After they had been married in the small Church, with only Annie present, weeping tears of happiness into her handkerchief, they had come back to eat a delicious meal.

It made them both remember the first dinner she and Annie had given "the Major," when the only food available had been a rabbit snared by Adam.

Tonight Annie had excelled herself with what she had already bought from the butcher to tempt Petula and the extras she sent Jason to procure for her.

As the Duke put his arms round Petula he said:

"I cannot help feeling amused, my darling one, when I have some very magnificent houses waiting for my wife, my Duchess, that we should start our married life in a cottage."

"Do you ... mind?" Petula enquired a little anxiously.

"Mind?" he replied. "It does not matter where I am as long as I am with you! And I think we shall always feel that Honeysuckle Cottage was a uniquely romantic place in which to begin our honeymoon."

"I was thinking in the wood before you came," Petula said, "that your wonderful kisses would be all I should have to ... remember in the future, but now ..."

It was impossible to find words for what she felt, and as if the Duke understood he kissed her very gently before he said:

"Buckden will have a very special place in our hearts, my darling, and perhaps we will come back here to revive the ecstasy we both felt when I first kissed you and when I knew today that I should never lose you."

He paused.

"And there will be another memory more precious than either of those."

His lips were on her hair as he said very softly:

"It is here, here in Buckden, in Honeysuckle Cottage, where I will make you mine completely and absolutely, now and for all time."

"I did not know it was . . . possible to be so . . . happy," Petula whispered.

"That is what I will make you," the Duke promised, "and, my darling, I am very impatient to show you how much I love you!"

Petula hid her face against him.

He held her close for a moment, then he put his fingers under her chin to look at her.

"You are so beautiful, so breathtakingly beautiful!" he said. "But my love for you is much more than that. As I have told you before and shall tell you again, you are part of me, and I cannot live without you."

He drew her close again as he went on:

"You are mine, Petula, mine not only for our whole lifetime together but for eternity and beyond. I believe that when a man and a woman are inseparably one, then where love is concerned there is no such thing as death."

"I thought when we were being . . . married that God had . . . brought us . . . together," Petula said breathlessly, "and nothing . . . nothing in the . . . whole Universe could . . . ever divide us."

She lifted her lips to the Duke's and he kissed her as if she was infinitely precious.

"I have not told you that Annie has . . . my father's . . . bed here," Petula said. "It was . . . where you . . . slept when you stayed at the Manor, and every night . . . I have thought of you and . . . pretended I was . . . in your arms."

"Tonight there will be no pretence," the Duke replied. "But must I wait much longer? I am tired of waiting for you, Petula, of being afraid of losing you and your enchantment."

There was a note of passion in his voice which made Petula feel wildly excited and yet at the same time very shy.

He felt her quiver and he said very softly:

"I want you! I want you, my darling. It is almost night, a night which will never be long enough for me."

Petula heard the yearning in his words and as she raised her face she whispered:

"I ... want you too! Will you ... come with ... me?"

She knew this was what the Duke wanted to hear; knew it by the sudden tightening of his arms, by the beating of his heart, by the fire she could see in his eyes.

Then with his arms round her and his lips on hers he drew her towards the door and up the twisting narrow staircase.

It led them into the small room which was filled with the great four-poster which had served the Buckdens faithfully for so many generations.

Overhead the stars came out one by one, there was only the shrill squeak of the bats and two voices murmuring over and over again:

"I love you! I love ... you!"

ABOUT THE AUTHOR

BARBARA CARTLAND, the world's most famous romantic novelist, who is also an historian, playwright, lecturer, political speaker and television personality, has now written over 200 books. She has also had many historical works published and has written four autobiographies as well as the biographies of her mother and that of her brother Ronald Cartland, who was the first Member of Parliament to be killed in the last war. This book has a preface by Sir Winston Churchill. Barbara Cartland has sold 80 million books over the world, more than half of these in the U.S.A. She broke the world record in 1975 by writing twenty books, and her own record in 1976 with twenty-one. In private life, Barbara Cartland, who is a Dame of the Order of St. John of Jerusalem, has fought for better conditions and salaries for Midwives and Nurses. As President of the Royal College of Midwives (Hertfordshire Branch), she has been invested with the first Badge of Office ever given in Great Britain, which was subscribed to by the Midwives themselves. She has also championed the cause for old people and founded the first Romany Gypsy Camp in the world. Barbara Cartland is deeply interested in Vitamin Therapy and is President of the British National Association for Health.

Barbara Cartland

The world's bestselling author of romantic fiction. Her stories are always captivating tales of intrigue, adventure and love.

☐	2107	A VERY NAUGHTY ANGEL	—$1.25
☐	2140	CALL OF THE HEART	—$1.25
☐	2147	AS EAGLES FLY	—$1.25
☐	2148	THE TEARS OF LOVE	—$1.25
☐	2149	THE DEVIL IN LOVE	—$1.25
☐	2436	THE ELUSIVE EARL	—$1.25
☐	2972	A DREAM FROM THE NIGHT	—$1.25
☐	10977	PUNISHMENT OF A VIXEN	—$1.50
☐	6387	THE PENNILESS PEER	—$1.25
☐	6431	LESSONS IN LOVE	—$1.25
☐	6435	THE DARING DECEPTION	—$1.25
☐	8103	CASTLE OF FEAR	—$1.25
☐	8240	THE RUTHLESS RAKE	—$1.25
☐	8280	THE DANGEROUS DANDY	—$1.25
☐	8467	THE WICKED MARQUIS	—$1.25
☐	11101	THE OUTRAGEOUS LADY	—$1.50
☐	11168	A TOUCH OF LOVE	—$1.50
☐	11169	THE DRAGON AND THE PEARL	—$1.50

Buy them at your local bookseller or use this handy coupon:

Bantam Books, Inc., Dept. BC, 414 East Golf Road, Des Plaines, Ill. 60016

Please send me the books I have checked above. I am enclosing $_____ (please add 50¢ to cover postage and handling). Send check or money order— no cash or C.O.D.'s please.

Mr/Mrs/Miss_____

Address_____

City_____ State/Zip_____

BC1—1/78

Please allow four weeks for delivery. This offer expires 7/78.

Barbara Cartland

The world's bestselling author of romantic fiction. Her stories are always captivating tales of intrigue, adventure and love.

☐	10972	LOOK, LISTEN AND LOVE	—$1.50
☐	10975	A DUEL WITH DESTINY	—$1.50
☐	10976	THE CURSE OF THE CLAN	—$1.50
☐	2366	THE MASK OF LOVE	—$1.25
☐	2426	AN ARROW OF LOVE	—$1.25
☐	2433	A KISS FOR THE KING	—$1.25
☐	2435	THE FRAGRANT FLOWER	—$1.25
☐	2450	FIRE ON THE SNOW	—$1.25
☐	2803	AN ANGEL IN HELL	—$1.25
☐	2804	THE WILD CRY OF LOVE	—$1.25
☐	2805	THE BLUE-EYED WITCH	—$1.25
☐	2806	THE INCREDIBLE HONEYMOON	—$1.25
☐	2950	THE SECRET OF THE GLEN	—$1.25
☐	2987	CONQUERED BY LOVE	—$1.25
☐	2993	NEVER LAUGH AT LOVE	—$1.25
☐	10337	HUNGRY FOR LOVE	—$1.25

Buy them at your local bookseller or use this handy coupon:

Barbara Cartland's Library of Love

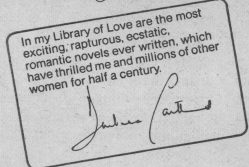

In my Library of Love are the most exciting, rapturous, ecstatic, romantic novels ever written, which have thrilled me and millions of other women for half a century.

Barbara Cartland

The World's Great Stories of Romance Specially Abridged by Barbara Cartland For Today's Readers.

☐	10927	THE WAY OF AN EAGLE by Ethel M. Dell	$1.50
☐	10926	THE REASON WHY by Elinor Glyn	$1.50
☐	10925	THE HUNDRETH CHANCE by Ethel M. Dell	$1.50
☐	10527	THE KNAVE OF DIAMONDS by Ethel M. Dell	$1.50
☐	10506	A SAFETY MATCH by Ian Hay	$1.50
☐	10498	HIS HOUR by Elinor Glyn	$1.50
☐	10497	THE SHEIK by E. M. Hull	$1.50
☐	11048	THE VICISSITUDES OF EVANGELINE by Elinor Glyn	$1.50
☐	11369	THE BARS OF IRON by Ethel M. Dell	$1.50
☐	11370	MAN AND MAID by Elinor Glyn	$1.50
☐	11391	THE SONS OF THE SHEIK by E. M. Hull	$1.50
☐	11376	SIX DAYS by Elinor Glyn	$1.50
☐	11466	RAINBOW IN THE SPRAY by Pamela Wayne	$1.50

Buy them at your local bookstore or use this handy coupon: